DEADLY BOUNTY

SCVC TASKFORCE ROMANTIC SUSPENSE
SERIES, BOOK 11

MISTY EVANS

Deadly Bounty, SCVC Taskforce Series, Book 11

Copyright © 2020 Misty Evans

Print ISBN: 978-1-948686-22-8

Cover Art by Fanderclai Design

Formatting by Beach Path Publishing, LLC

Editing by Elizabeth Neal, Patricia Essex

Please Note

1

———

*S*an Diego

The woman watched from the cover of the trees as Joseph Cahill, bounty hunter, left his vehicle under a streetlight.

He glanced both ways and pressed his key fob. The BMW's lights flickered twice, letting him know it was locked. Casually, he meandered into the building that housed a senior center and a private accounting firm.

Joe was a bruiser of a guy, a weight lifter and former college football star. Nearing thirty, time hadn't diminished his size or the perpetual hard expression on his face. The tattoos on his arms, visible under his black T-shirt, looked as menacing as his countenance.

Perspiration trickled down her back as she watched him disappear inside, her blouse sticking to the skin along her spine. Today, the temp had hit a hundred degrees, causing people on the street to collapse from heat exhaustion in record numbers.

In the hazy evening light, things were a bit cooler, but she had to admit not all of her sweat was due to the awful July heat. At least some was from irrepressible fear.

Three weeks and two days since the incident—boy, how things had changed. She'd never dreamed she'd be here, on the run. Her life had become chaos, completely out of her control, and no one believed she was innocent.

And she had no idea why Joe—the number one fugitive apprehension agent in the country—was going inside *this* location.

He was too young to be a member of the senior center and doubtful he was invited to the apparent party they were throwing. She'd seen multiple men and women coming and going in bright clothing, carrying various types of food.

The accounting firm was probably closed, but she could be wrong. Maybe, for some reason, he'd driven from Carlsbad to San Diego to speak to a bookkeeper...yeah, that seemed likely.

He was the perfect person for Homeland and the Feds to send after her. Everything had gone to hell in a handbasket on July 4th. All she'd worked so hard for destroyed with the bomb.

Local law enforcement had been the first to grab her, and she'd been completely blindsided at first, otherwise she would've been on the run the minute the explosion happened.

The FBI had stepped in, yet she'd been convinced she could straighten out the misconception she'd had something to do with the bombing that had rocked an Independence Day parade. Yes, the man who'd done it was one of her undercover contacts, but there'd been no reason to believe *she* was the mastermind behind the attack.

It all still seemed surreal, as if someone had kicked her in the gut, even after being on the run these past weeks. How could anyone believe she—Samantha Rosenthal, FBI agent and undercover operative—would commit terrorism?

Hell, she'd never drawn her gun on the job, and she'd faced

a multitude of dangerous criminals. To believe she could plant a bomb to hurt all those innocent people...

A shudder went through her. Escaping her fellow agents hadn't been easy, but she'd been raised by spies. Her mother and father had been CIA operatives, and she herself had been top of her class at Quantico.

She'd grown up with three brothers which hadn't hurt either. Learning evasion and escape techniques, thanks to all those components, had served her well.

Her first thought had been to go to her mom for aid in straightening out this horrible misunderstanding. That would be the first place her coworkers would look, and she couldn't drag her family into this mess.

Two of her brothers were out of the country, both government employees themselves, and the third was at MIT, working on his second degree. None of them would believe the reports about her, and they were all probably searching for her, too, but involving any of them in this was a no-go.

A group of three boys went by on the sidewalk, one on a skateboard. They were talking about a baseball phenom and the number of balls he'd launched out of the park in the All-Star Home Run Derby.

Sam had considered going to her old friend, Olivia Fiorelli. They'd known each other since they were kids, and Olivia was now a US Marshal. Samantha had given two Marshals the slip, and dropping in on Olivia to beg for help when her organization was in on the manhunt, along with the FBI and Homeland, was also out of the question. Olivia was a good friend, and she was happy now. The last Sam heard from her, before all of this had happened, she was planning a fall wedding to West Coast FBI Director Victor Dupé.

That left Sam with one option...and not a good one.

Joe.

He was well acquainted with her work ethic and complete

and utter devotion to her country—a perfect match for his. Like her mother, he had to know she'd never do what they claimed. He would believe her.

Wouldn't he?

Reaching out was extremely uncomfortable, and not just because of her current situation. She'd been in love with him, planned to marry him, in fact. But things went south after he left the FBI to join his older brothers' bail bond agency.

Sam's dreams of the future had gotten sidetracked, and suddenly Joe was constantly on the road, out of touch. He grew unhappy when she accepted a role in the new counterterrorism taskforce, requiring her to do long-term undercover work. Harsh words had been said; their loving relationship had turned into a battlefield. Her heart still hurt every time she thought of him and the love that had been snuffed out.

Her job had been to get close to people whom profilers identified as radical enough to commit a terrorist crime within a year. She hadn't been allowed to tell anyone about the beta program or the top secret group she'd been assigned to, not even Joe. It had been the last straw for him, forcing her to choose between their relationship and her work.

Jimmy T, the parade bomber, had been her most recent target.

The beta software used to flag the high risk potential terrorists had been designed by a genius kid at USC working on his doctorate. Quiet Streets, it was labeled. Her mark had been on that list, and had a thing for brunettes with sassy mouths. So that's what she'd become to insert herself into his pathetic, but often violent, life. It wasn't much of a stretch.

Taking out terrorists made Sam's pulse beat a little faster. Made her feel as if she was doing something to protect her country. Going undercover was simply slipping on another persona, and came with ease.

She'd played with her mother's disguises when she was a

girl, overheard her parents discuss operations where they'd altered not only their appearance, but had to remember challenging backstop identities, and use other languages as they pretended to be from different countries. It had sounded like a fascinating game to her.

Growing up to become an undercover agent was a dream come true.

Joe thought she was reckless, that there were other agents who could do the work. He'd told her Kyle Dunmire's software program was walking a fine line, identifying suspects before they'd actually committed any crime. He was big on free will.

He hadn't agreed with any of it, and she'd been frustrated with his short-sightedness. Random domestic terrorist bombings had been on the rise the past two years. She was determined to put a stop to them, and prevention was always better, wasn't it?

In Sam's mind, there was no one hundred percent cure, but she would do whatever it took to thwart their selfish acts of violence.

A lot of good that ideology had done her. Now, here she was, unable to prove her innocence and on the run from the entire world.

An elderly couple emerged arm in arm, laughing, and swaying slightly on their feet. At least the woman was. The man, while moving slowly and struggling to keep his balance against his companion's teetering, seemed to be sober enough to drive. He tucked his wife—girlfriend?—in the front of an old Pontiac and hobble-walked to the driver's side. He took his time getting in, putting on his seatbelt, and starting it.

As they drove off, Sam had another gut check. She'd believed in love and happily-ever-after. Her dreams of growing old with Joe still lodged deeply in her heart. Outside of protecting her country, and being a good daughter, it's all she'd ever wanted.

He was all she'd ever wanted.

Shoving the thought aside, she forced her attention back to the front of the building. Maybe she could sneak in, figure out where he'd gone, and why.

She was about to exit the car she'd recently stolen from a used dealership, when a black SUV wheeled in and took the spot the old man had vacated. As the driver hopped out and scanned the area, Sam crouched down lower, even though he couldn't see her.

Her blood went cold.

Dr. Roman Walsh, head of the Domestic Terrorism Taskforce and a Homeland agent high up the chain of command.

Why was he in San Diego? Specifically, what in the hell was he doing here?

She'd met him briefly while working on Quiet Streets. He had one of his people on the team, along with Sam and several more agents.

Seeing him, pieces of this black hole puzzle fell into place. He was meeting Joe.

The bounty hunter.

Fugitive apprehension agent, he'd correct her. He hated the term bounty hunter.

Walsh was a different side of the same coin. His team was looking for her, like the rest of law enforcement, and he'd figured out she and Joe had once had a relationship. It wasn't a secret.

Again, Sam felt that drop in her belly. After three-plus weeks, the government was seeking outside help to bring a federal fugitive to justice.

Joe's specialty.

His brothers used him for cases the government wanted to keep under wraps. In particular, when people from the alphabet agencies—NSA, FBI, CIA, etc.—went dark and tried to disappear.

She shouldn't be surprised they'd recruited Joe, but she was kind of shocked he'd agreed.

Dammit all to hell. Had Joe actually accepted the task of bringing her in?

Walsh entered the building, holding the door for a pair of elderly ladies exiting. One of them lit a cigarette as soon as she hit the sidewalk.

Sam knew it was dangerous, but she waited for them to mosey off before she crossed the street. What was it about this place that brought the two men here? They could've discussed the assignment on the phone, met for coffee or a beer.

Had they realized *she* was in San Diego?

She had to know, and more importantly, ascertain if Joe was working for the enemy.

One of the problems about being on the run in Southern California in late July was she couldn't wear bulky clothes or hide under a hood. She had a ball cap with a wig underneath, and sunglasses, but she was still a sitting duck.

The women, both of whom had to be in their seventies, were arguing in the parking lot. Sam, head lowered, slipped into the shadows.

As she waited for them to get in their car, she heard the front door open. Two people emerged—a man and a woman, the woman talking into a cell, low but urgent. "No, we need to get that warrant tonight. Yes, I'm aware it's nearly nine, but this can't wait."

Side by side, they hurried down the block and Sam caught sight of them in more detail as they passed the skinny alley. Long shadows fell across the street, but the woman's smooth, dark skin, and abundant afro stood out.

Ronni Punto. *Agent* Ronni Punto.

She looked more like a model than a decorated FBI agent. Her partner was Thomas Mann, another agent.

The black hole shitfest expanded.

They worked for the Southern California Violent Crimes Taskforce.

Joe...Walsh...the Taskforce.

Samantha's insides liquified, her stomach bottoming out.

This had to be a covert meeting place for the SCVC. If Walsh had called Joe here, they were all working together.

To bring her in.

I don't stand a chance.

Her last and final hope was her ex, but it seemed her worst fear had come to pass.

Joe was now the enemy.

2

Somedays his job sucked.

Joe was a natural when it came to catching fugitives. His twin brothers had started Bondsman Brothers after leaving the Marines, and they hired veterans who couldn't find decent work in other professions.

They'd nagged him for years to join them, and he'd blown them off. He'd loved the Bureau, finding his niche in kidnapping and missing persons. Once when Caleb and Malachi were shorthanded, he'd given in and accepted a skip trace assignment—just a one-time gig. The hunt got into his blood, and now, thanks to that, his back was against the wall.

What the hell were you thinking, Sam?

Joe checked his watch—it was just after ten. He and Roman Walsh walked the hall, having completed their meeting with Cooper Harris and his taskforce. Samantha Rosenthal, charged with conspiring against the U.S. government, and a handful of others, had broken free during a Bureau transfer from San Diego to Los Angeles and gone on the run. Marshals had caught her, then lost her again. The last sighting was in Southern California, near the border.

She was good, but as far as they could determine, she hadn't crossed into Mexico. Why, he didn't know. After the bombing, why hadn't she vamoosed across the border and kept going?

The Beach Boys filtered through the open door of the senior center. One of the spry elderly gals hustled out when she saw them, calling, "You boys looking for a little fun tonight?"

He and Walsh exchanged a look, and the DTT leader, always savvy and charming to women no matter their age, winked at the gal. "If we weren't on the hunt for a big, bad terrorist, we'd join you. Have fun."

Joe didn't miss the woman's eyeroll. She had no idea he was telling the truth. The taskforce met here under the guise of a support group, and she probably assumed they were avoiding the party to stay sober.

"Is that so?" she asked as they continued. "Sure. I hope you catch him!"

Him. The man driving the truck filled with explosives had died in the bombing. The person behind it—at least according to the higher sources of the US government—was a little petite thing, barely over five-four and a hundred-and-ten pounds soaking wet, who talked in her sleep and liked to be kissed behind her left earlobe...

There wasn't much he didn't know about her, like the fact she was highly intelligent, calculating, and extremely efficient at evasion.

His chest squeezed with remorse every time he thought of her.

Night had fully fallen, the heat from the sidewalk hitting them full force as they exited the building. Walsh slapped him on the shoulder. "With you helping Harris and the others, we should have her by the end of the week."

Right. Because if there was anyone Sam might reach out to, it was him. Not her family—she was too smart to do that. But her ex? A sure bet.

And didn't that make him feel incredibly good on one hand, and like a piece of shit on the other.

She's too smart to contact me, either, he reassured himself.

He told himself the cramp in his belly was due to the heat and humidity, but deep down, it was that five-foot four firecracker upsetting his digestion.

Damn woman had broken his heart. Now she was testing the depth of emotions he'd had for her all this time.

The head of the Domestic Terrorism Taskforce sauntered toward his SUV, leaving Joe on the sidewalk. He stood there a moment longer, watching the taillights flicker as Walsh drove away. It was all men on deck now, women, too. Everyone up and down the state of California was determined to bring Sam to justice.

Him included, now that Homeland had roped him in.

It wasn't as if he could refuse, which was another hellish thing about this whole pickle.

He couldn't believe she'd blow up anything. She was no terrorist. Not the Sam he knew.

But did he *really* know her after all these months?

Had he ever? That was the bigger question, adding to his indigestion. If not, she'd duped him, along with a whole lot of other people.

He shook his head. Rubbed the spot on his chest where it felt like he'd been shot. He had in a sense—his heart ripped clean out. He was never getting Sam out of his system, and he cursed himself for it.

The worst part? If she *did* come and want him to go on the run with her? He'd do it in a heartbeat. No questions asked.

That's how much of a weakness she was for him.

He'd also have to say it. *I told you so.* She hadn't heeded his warnings and now they'd come true.

If she was actually innocent. He had no way of knowing.

Outside the driver of that truck, no one had died that day,

but there were over a dozen injuries. The fairground had been packed with people to watch the parade and enjoy the fireworks when the sun went down. He'd almost been there himself, but had wrapped up an arduous apprehension only a few hours earlier. All he'd wanted was a homecooked meal and a decent eight hours of sleep.

Fishing his keys from his pocket, he wiped sweat from the back of his neck and ambled toward his car. The opposing sides of his brain—and his heart—warred like an angel and a devil on his shoulders. One tried to convince him she was innocent. The other, cataloging the evidence, insisted on her guilt.

The car lights flashed as he unlocked the door and climbed in. He stuck the key in the ignition, looking up just in time to catch movement in the backseat.

Instinct made him jump, reaching for his weapon, when a soft female voice said, "I don't want to hurt you. I just came to talk."

Shock slid down his spine. He hadn't heard that voice since New Year's Day.

He jerked around. "Sam?" The overhead streetlight had been broken out long ago and never replaced; the backseat a tapestry of shadows. Faint illumination from down the street threw a slash of light across her eyes and high cheekbones. She wore a ball cap and her hair looked different. "What the hell?"

"I didn't do it. You know I'm innocent, right?"

He swallowed the tightness in his throat. "My god, I can't believe you're here."

"Me either."

He wished he could stare at her for the rest of the night, soak her in, but this was a volatile situation. The edge of a knife for him—and her. "They've hired me to bring you in."

Not exactly a vote of confidence, and he saw her lips twist in irritation. "I know. I have to say I'm a little disappointed you took the job."

He couldn't see any weapon, and he held the belief she wouldn't hurt him, but it didn't make him feel exactly safe. She might not be the 'big, bad terrorist' that came to mind at that description, but she was certainly capable of inflicting great pain if she chose to.

"Tell me your side," he said smoothly, hoping to sound like the trusted friend he still wanted to be for her. "And for the record, they didn't give me a choice about this. *You* didn't either. Obviously, Homeland and the Feds came to me, believing I have the inside scoop."

"Of course. You do." She was so still, so composed, it made him nervous. Her eyes shifted to the building and checked the street before returning to his. "I need you to look into a grad student at USC."

Disable her. Find a way to take her in, tonight, before anyone else gets hurt.

Especially her. "What does he have to do with this?"

"The whole thing was a setup." Her eyes were sincere, earnest. "I don't have time to explain it right now, but I need to find out if his computer program flagged *me* as a potential terrorist. I believe that's why the Bureau actually thinks I did this. I'd investigate that angle myself, but as you can guess, my access to anyone and anything connected is extremely restricted at the moment."

There was a touch of sarcasm in her voice, but he also heard exhaustion, disbelief.

Some people could stay on the run for years, others didn't have it in them. He was pretty sure if she made it through another few weeks, she would for the rest of her life.

What kind of life would that be?

Ask me, he found himself mentally urging. *Ask me to go with you.*

Her face was calm, unsettling, but nothing in it held an invitation to head to Mexico. He shifted forward, slowly, so as not to startle her, regrouping. There was a stun gun within reach if he could manage to distract her.

"Let's go to my place and you can tell me everything. When was the last time you had a decent meal?" He started the car, ready to surreptitiously reach under the seat.

She sat forward and grabbed the door handle. "I'd love to take you up on that, Joe, but I can't trust you at the moment. Oh, and by the way, it's not under there."

Goddamn. Of course she'd already searched the vehicle and taken his weapon. He glanced in the rearview. "You're not going to zap me, are you?"

A smile crossed her lips. It was thin and brief, without humor. "There are several reasons I'd like to tase your ass, but no, I didn't come here to exact revenge over old grievances. I know I'm asking a lot, but I don't have anywhere else to turn. I was framed. I don't know who was behind it, and I don't know why. I have to start somewhere, and the minute I try to get close to Kyle Dunmire, they'll nab me. He's under surveillance and doesn't even know it. Genius when it comes to computers, but not a lick of street smarts."

Joe considered hitting the door lock, hoping the child safety was on in the backseat. He would trap her inside, start the car, and take off. She wouldn't tase him, fearing he'd crash.

She was too quick, knowing him as well as he knew himself. Shoving the door open, she quickly exited, tapping the back of his head with the end of the Taser. "I'll let you return to your bounty hunting. Just please, think about what I said. I know this means putting your job on the line to help me, but I swear, I was *not* behind that bombing. If you could give me more time, help me run down a couple leads, that's all I'm asking. Just check into it, and see if you don't think it's extremely suspicious that the guy I was supposed to stop from doing this is dead, and they've pinned it all on me. You know me, Joe."

The last words were said very quietly as she stood outside. "I would never do something like this. Never."

The angel and devil on his shoulders went to war again. *She's innocent, tell her you believe her. She's guilty, don't let her get away.*

As he struggled about what to do, his firecracker gave him a sad smile and disappeared into the night.

3

S am slunk into the shadows, quickly becoming one herself, before Joe could follow.

As expected, he exited the BMW, yelling her name into the night, as she ran on silent feet.

A few more yards, and she crouched at her lookout point and reached for her binoculars.

She studied him, feasting on his hard face and muscular body. The earnestness in his features was obvious, even though the light and shadows playing across them added to his menacing air. As he turned in circles, scanning, she saw glints of light off his rich, dark hair and wished she could run her hands through it.

His mouth formed a hard line, frustration oozing from every pore of his body. He kicked out with one foot, slamming the backseat door shut.

Sam *tsked* under her breath. "That's no way to treat a lady," she murmured softly. He must be especially mad at not getting his collar if he was kicking his baby.

A car cruised by on the street between her hiding place and Joe's vehicle. He regained his composure, closed his door, and went to the trunk to retrieve a flashlight. Sam smiled as he took time to carefully shine it over and under the car.

Smart. He knew the only way she could've trailed him here was if she'd stuck a tracking unit on the Beemer, which meant she was one step ahead of him. He'd never noticed how close she'd been, and he hated it when she got the upper hand.

They'd always been two damn good agents at heart, always trying to get the best of each other.

In and out of bed.

He found the first, dropped it on the sidewalk and stomped on it. At the same time, the head of the SCVC Taskforce exited the building.

Cooper Harris, nicknamed The Beast, fit the moniker well. He was a big guy—football player sized like Joe—and he went on alert as soon as he noticed Joe still there, squashing something under his foot.

"Everything okay?" Harris called.

Sam tensed, waiting for him to spill the beans. To admit that the woman they were all chasing had surprised him in his own vehicle after planting a tracking device on it.

Worse, she'd been within inches of him, and yet, he'd been unable to make the arrest. He could be a hero right now. Instead, he was faced with admitting failure.

"Cockroach." Joe's eyes scanned in her direction. She forced herself not to move or even breathe. There was no way he could see her, no way he could know she was there. She stayed immobile anyway.

Uncannily, his gaze seemed to lock on hers for a long, tense moment. Then it moved on.

Sam let out a slow breath.

The two men said their goodbyes, Harris telling Joe to call if he got any leads.

Joe nodded. "You'll be the first to know," he promised, before getting in his car.

Sam silently thanked Harris for the diversion. Joe hadn't gone back to searching for another device, and she never planted only one. She'd hidden the second inside the vehicle.

A part of her hoped the reason he hadn't told Harris about her was because he was still loyal to her on some level. After all they'd been through working together in their professional lives and falling in love, it wasn't too farfetched. He'd stood by her when Alison Kendrick had stalked him and caused all kinds of problems for her. He'd been the shoulder she cried on when she failed to obtain her first promotion. He'd gone home with her when her father died and been her rock through the funeral and afterwards.

She still had the diamond he'd proposed with, but it was back in her apartment in L.A. She'd give anything to have it on her finger right now. Wondered what might've happened if they'd married as intended.

Joe drove off, and knowing him, she stayed put a while longer. He'd cruise the streets, accosting people and asking if they'd seen her. He was a bulldog when he was after something, which made him perfect for his job. Even with his size and demeanor, he had no trouble making friends with folks and motivating them to help him.

He should have been a spy.

She wasn't one to sit still long, but she forced herself to for thirty minutes. She watched the app on her burner phone—a necessity once she'd lost all of her personal electronics—to track the GPS. Eventually, it showed Joe moving from the area and heading north.

Hot and tired, she climbed into the stolen vehicle, drove to a different lot, and traded it. This was part of her process— hitting small-time used car lots, breaking into the office, lifting the key and a dealer's plate, and replacing her wheels.

The transfer took a few minutes longer because she had supplies to move from the old to the new, but she was on her way in less than fifteen minutes and headed for the deserted bridge by the water.

Out of habit, she drove randomly for another half hour, making sure no one tailed her. Once she felt sure she was in the clear, she drove to the closest abandoned building and parked.

Tourists were easy to lift items from. Many came from far distances and simply purchased what they wanted for their beach excursions once they were in town. Some left those same items behind, others weren't careful about guarding them when they were out and about.

Tonight, she had a fancy cooler on wheels that still had ice and chilled beverages in it. She slung a beach bag over her shoulder that contained several towels, two souvenir t-shirts, sunscreen, and a pair of sunglasses. From inside Joe's car, she'd absconded with a couple twenties, a few ones, and change. She'd pocketed it all.

The half-moon reclined on its back in the sky as she made her way through the scrub and sand to the waterfront. This was no nice beach; it smelled like rotting vegetation and chemicals. A compact fire burned in a metal drum, and Hetty was warming her hands over it, even though Sam was sweating with the effort of walking a few blocks.

The petite Asian woman in her fifties was always cold. Probably because she didn't get to eat much, and was skinny as the handle on the cooler.

"Brought you some goodies," Sam called, smiling at the way the woman's eyes lit up.

A scruffy dog jumped up from a pile of blankets several feet on the other side of the fire and rushed her, barking. The muscular terrier mix tried to appear quite fierce, but as soon as he recognized her, Jack-Jack wagged his tail so hard he nearly fell over.

"Brought you something too, boy." From her pocket, she

withdrew a package of beef jerky—another thing she'd lifted from Joe.

Some things never change. Energy drinks and beef jerky—the man lived on both. She never understood how he could look so buff when he existed on sugar and salted meat.

Jack-Jack ran off with the jerky, still wagging, and plopped himself on the blankets to inhale the food. Hetty groaned as she stood from her box chair and limped to the cooler and tote. Her eyes were bright and her smile big as she clapped her hands together. "It's like finding treasure," she whispered into the night.

Hetty was missing a tooth here and there, but the smile warmed Sam's heart. She handed her the beach bag. "I want you to start using the sunscreen in here all over your face, okay? There are also shirts I think will fit you."

Unceremoniously, Hetty turned the bag over and dumped the contents on the sand. She looked each item over carefully, holding it toward the fire as if to scrutinize the haul in detail.

"Where's Dec?" Sam asked.

Hetty never said much, and she stuck to that, motioning with a gnarled finger toward a shadow under a tree. Sam squinted to make out Dec's pop-up tent. "Hey, Dec," she called. "Come get something to drink."

Hetty, wanting to make sure she got first dibs, tossed down the shirt she'd been holding and tugged at the lid. Sam opened it and Hetty made a noise in the back of her throat that sounded like delight. Arthritic fingers grabbed a bottle of Mountain Dew. "Your sugar daddy give you this?" she asked in accented English.

Sam chuckled. "If I had a sugar daddy, do you think I'd be running around under this bridge, hanging out with you losers?"

Hetty liked to trade insults, and at first, it had caught Sam off guard when she'd hurled one at her. The woman's life caused her to rely on lighthearted verbal abuse in order to get through her days. Their teasing banter, since Sam had joined her and Dec, had brought a little spark to Sam's heart.

"You like us better than *normal* assholes," Hetty said, and Sam couldn't argue the fact.

Here, she wasn't a terrorist on the run. She was just Sam, who regularly brought Hetty and Declyn a few meager things to make their existence slightly less traumatic.

The tall, skinny young man crawled from his tent, stood and yawned. As he walked toward them, shirtless, he stretched his arms over head. One was shrunken compared to the other, an accident he'd told her. He had little use of it from the elbow down, and no luck scrounging up a job. His personality didn't fit with *normal assholes* either.

"Santa Claus came again?" He offered a sideways grin.

Sam made Hetty share. Dec took pieces of the melting ice and rubbed it around the back of his neck.

They sat and talked, drank and laughed, calling each other silly names and staring at the oily, polluted water washing up on the scant piece of shore. Sam would've killed for a shower and a bed, but everything was standing in her way of those two simple things that made life so much nicer.

She thought about calling Frank, her boss. If she could just leave a message, tell him to look into...what? Where was the evidence proving she was innocent? What could she say to convince him she'd been set up?

Frank had believed in her, and she could imagine he was kicking himself for that now. There were others, too. Agents she'd gone undercover with, preached loyalty and duty to.

As her mates tucked themselves in for the night, Sam stayed near the fire watching it burn down to embers. Jack-Jack came and sat next to her legs, the stray having attached himself to her the moment she arrived at this paltry camp and bribed these two to allow her to join them.

From her back pocket, she withdrew a list of names, reading them for the hundredth time. They were the only people who had access, means, and a potential motive to send her undercover to recruit a terrorist, then turn the tables on her.

She'd given Joe the first, not because the USC student was a mastermind who could've pulled all of this off, but he was the one in position to have had contact with the person who *was*.

As the fire eventually went out, Sam's eyelids grew heavy. Another day on the run, but she was alive, and perhaps she'd made the smallest bit of progress.

Her head filled with images of Joe, she returned her list to the pocket, patted Jack-Jack on the head, and closed her eyes.

$$4$$

The cold water of the shower felt like pins and needles on his skin. Bracing a hand against the tile, Joe leaned into it. He needed to wake up his mind after only two hours of sleep and calm his lower half where his morning erection was hard enough to drill holes in the wall.

Both were thanks to his ex. Seven months and twenty-eight days—twenty-nine now—since she'd moved out, leaving his heart, and future, in tatters.

The past day had bled into this one, his night spent canvassing the streets for her unsuccessful. She was once again in the wind. He'd stopped every person he'd come across, flashing pictures from his personal collection on his phone. Those individuals who weren't afraid of him gave him the same response—they hadn't seen her.

They might have, but with her disguise, they didn't recognize her from his photos.

He'd visited all the spots street people hung out. Since working as an apprehension agent, he'd grown accustomed to night work, hunting his prey in the shadows. She had to be living on the streets. It was risky to still be in the country, but if she was determined to prove her innocence, she couldn't do that if she bailed.

He soaped his hair and body and was in the middle of rinsing when he heard a dog bark. Just a couple of yips that immediately put him on alert. He left the water running, wiped his eyes, and threw a towel around his waist. His Beretta was on the counter, and he snatched it up and flipped off the safety.

The condo development was small-scale, with only a dozen units. The landlord didn't allow animals, and unless the dog was right outside his door, Joe shouldn't hear it so clearly.

It wasn't. He listened at the bathroom door, only half closed, and heard someone moving in the kitchen.

On wet but silent feet, he crept from the bathroom, crossed the bedroom floor, and leaned out to look down the hall. A shadow moved near the breakfast bar, and he heard the clink of a cup on the counter.

Shit. There was only one person who would break into his place at six in the morning and make herself coffee.

A new alertness came over him, and at the same time, his shoulders relaxed. Taking a deep breath and reining in the urge to tackle her, he reminded himself this could be a critical turning point. He'd lost her last night, and he wasn't about to have a repeat.

As he walked down the hall and entered the kitchen, he found the source of the barking—a dirty mutt with crazy hair stood on all fours and curled his lip at him.

Leaning against the counter, Sam looked as tired as Joe felt, her dark eyes watching him over the rim of a cup. The smell of the fresh brewed coffee penetrated his nose, and then his brain, clearing some of the cobwebs. Underneath that aroma, he caught the odor of wet dog.

For a long moment, he simply stood and stared at Sam,

taking her in. The morning light filtering through the kitchen window gave him a much better view than he'd had yesterday.

She looked thin, too thin. A tightness set in around her mouth when she finished sipping.

He rubbed his forehead with his free hand, keeping the gun loose in the other next to his side. "Are you out of your goddamn mind?"

"Good morning to you, too," she replied. "Coffee?"

There wasn't enough of the stuff in the world to offset the headache beginning to pound between his temples. "Marshals have my place under surveillance, you know."

She withdrew a second mug from the cabinet, the kitchen as familiar as her own to her. A trip to his side-by-side and she removed the creamer, dumped some into the cup, then poured coffee in. As she slid it across the breakfast bar, she said, "No one saw us."

The dog continued snarling at him, so he set down the Glock and accepted the coffee. As if sensing the all-clear, the beast wagged its tail ever so slightly.

"The only reason I took this job was to make sure nobody else caught you and brought you in."

She arched a brow and went back to her drink. Her gaze started at his wet hair, dropped to his jawline, and lowered to his chest. She took in his shoulders, his biceps, his hands—a slow, tantalizing appraisal.

Her focus returned to his chest—a feature she'd always been fascinated with—and he couldn't resist, expanding his pecs to make sure he gave her a show.

Finally, she lifted her eyes to meet his. "Good to hear you say that, although you're not bringing me in either."

He huffed, setting the cup down a bit too hard. The mutt went back to snarling at him. "You want to call off your attack dog?"

"No. And he's not mine. He doesn't belong to anyone."

Kind of like me, her eyes seemed to echo. She covered it up quickly by glancing away.

"This complex doesn't allow dogs." It seemed like an inane thing to say at the moment, since she already knew that, but anything to keep her talking and present in his kitchen was worth a try. "Better hope the neighbors don't call the manager."

She gave a one-shoulder shrug. "We won't be here long."

"Why *are* you here?"

She was dressed in layers too warm for the day and he wondered if she was packing his stun gun. "I'm going with you to talk to Kyle."

After getting the okay from Dupé, Joe had reached out to the USC grad student, still in town for summer classes, and was meeting him this morning. "The hell you are. You're a wanted felon, Sammie. You can't walk up and start interrogating him. First of all, they're watching him in case you might do exactly that. You said so yourself. Secondly, you'd scare the shit out of him and he wouldn't tell you a damn thing."

"I'll stay out of sight, but you need me running backup."

"Bullshit. If I needed backup, I'd call Harris, which I don't, by the way."

Pleading eyes locked on his. She had a sweet, innocent air about her when she wanted to, and men were suckers for those big brown eyes, like fish going after a worm on a hook.

At his silence, she pressed her lips together and sighed. "I can handle it."

"You're not going anywhere near this kid."

"Always so bossy." The dog moved closer, no longer showing his fangs, and sniffed at Joe. The tail wagged a little.

"I need to coach you." She switched gears. "You don't even know what to ask."

"Look, you could use a shower and a decent meal. My offer stands. Clean yourself up, I'll make breakfast, then you can write down your questions. I'm going to his place at ten-thirty."

She gave him a benevolent smile. "Nice try. I need to be there since I may have to steer the conversation, based on the replies he gives you. You don't know enough about the undercover work and his software's role in what I was doing."

He leaned on the counter, placing both hands on the cool surface in order to keep from shaking sense into her. Clearing his throat, he attempted to keep the exasperation from his voice. Failed. "Coach me right here. Explain it all so I understand."

The dog backed off again, sensing his irritation and went to stand by Sam, putting his thirty-pound body in front of her as if to protect her.

She patted him, scratching between his ears. "I'm not even sure I understand what all the software can do, and it would take too much time to explain all the ins and outs of it. That's why we need to talk to Kyle. Together."

Joe straightened, put his hands on his hips, and took a small amount of pride when her eyes dropped to his chest again. "If you want me to get to the bottom of this, you have to trust me. Like I said, you can give me the fundamentals over breakfast, and if anything raises a flag when I talk to him, I'll text you. I assume you have a cell."

"If they're surveilling your place, they're also keeping tabs on your phones—landline and cell. I suppose we could get a burner for you…" She stopped, seeming to think it over, and shook her head. Snapped her fingers. "A listening device. Earbuds. I can hear what he's saying and I'll coach you through them."

She wasn't gonna let this go. "You'll still have to be closer than I want for that to work."

Returning the creamer, she snagged a loaf of bread. Two slices went in the toaster and she refilled her cup. "I suggest you get dressed. We have a lot to talk about before we go."

The dog sat next to the stove, his eyes on Joe. "Scramble

some eggs for you and the dog," he said, picking up his gun and coffee. "I'll be back in a minute."

Any sane man would call Harris or Walsh.

Instead, he found himself in his office. There, he rummaged through his stock of equipment, gathering a body mic and a set of earbuds.

5

———

Kyle Dunmire lived three blocks from the college in a neighborhood designated for off-campus housing. Shabby couches decorated front porches of two-story homes converted to apartments. Red plastic cups and beer bottles, casually tossed aside after a night of drinking, decorated front lawns and steps.

Kyle's apartment was on the upper floor of such a house in a nicer area. His downstairs neighbor was gone for the summer, leaving the apartment vacant. Sam had driven by it before, considering the idea of confronting him, or sneaking in to inspect his software.

It wasn't like she could sit down and have a cup of coffee with the guy. Even with a disguise, her pointed questions would reveal her true identity in minutes.

Breaking in while he was gone and having a look at his computer—most likely provided by the government—wouldn't do much good either. She could search his software and databases all day and not understand exactly how either worked. Nor would that help her figure out who was behind the bombing.

Someone on the Quiet Streets Taskforce? Or higher up? The list of names—people she'd put her life on the line for—burned in her back pocket.

A single Marshal kept watch over Kyle's place and Sam made sure to stay out of sight of the unmarked car. She'd avoided the one watching Joe's this morning, the guy asleep when she snuck in to surprise her former lover.

After convincing Joe to allow her to shadow him, a wire in place on his gorgeous chest so she could listen to the conversation, she'd spotted the Marshal leaving his spot to venture to the Quik-Mart down the road. She's been watching him for three days, and he'd done the same thing the previous two mornings, using the restroom and grabbing a donut and coffee.

If she were still an active agent, she would have turned him in to Olivia for being so sloppy, but he probably hated this assignment and doubted she would show up at Joe's so early in the morning. He was wrong on that account.

Excited about the plan, and the fact Joe had finally relented to her tagging along, Sam had slipped and given him a quick kiss out of habit. He'd looked as startled as she'd felt at her gaffe, but knew better than to say anything.

Her lips still tingled from the kiss. It had been totally spontaneous, catching both of them off guard. For one awkward moment, she'd nearly laughed. But before Joe could say anything, or the sexual magnetism between them could fully explode, she'd bailed, leaving Jack-Jack safe in the condo.

Could she be held responsible for losing her head for a moment after what she'd been through in the past few weeks?

No, but she couldn't excuse the fact she wanted to kiss him again.

Tightening her grip on her binoculars, she shoved the thought away, and focused on Kyle's place across the street. Time to get her head back in the game.

She'd prepped Joe as much as she could and hoped it'd be

enough. Computer programming was above her pay grade—she needed answers to questions, not a coding lesson. She sure hoped Joe could get them.

While he was in the shower, she'd helped herself to several of the toys he kept stashed in his office. She hadn't let him know she planned to sneak in and leave a few bugs in Kyle's apartment while Joe kept him busy. Maybe even a camera or two. It was a long shot as far as unraveling what had happened to her, but one she needed to start with in order to follow a trail...one that so far had eluded her.

Of course, she'd been just a tad busy avoiding the police, FBI, Homeland, the Marshals, and a host of general citizens determined to find her and turn her in.

There had to be a trail. Nobody could orchestrate this type of operation without leaving fingerprints or bread-crumbs along the way. If she could keep Joe on her side chasing the mystery with her, she might be able to figure it out.

And if she could, she had the feeling it would lead to another, even bigger unraveling that was going to be all kinds of ugly. She'd been circling that for over a year, trying to get Frank to let her dig deeper. He'd shut her down every time, saying she had no concrete evidence, and when she'd threatened to go up the chain-of-command, she'd nearly gotten fired for insubordination. Frank adored her, but could only be pushed so far.

Joe arrived a few minutes after she was in position down the street on the top floor of a similar house-turned-apartment with her binoculars. This particular living quarters was vacant as well, thanks to it being summer, and she had a view of the Marshal watching Kyle's, as well as the panorama up and down the street.

An overgrown hedge and a dilapidated garage hid the back entry to Kyle's. The neighbors were also college grads who did a lot of partying and had a vampire-ish schedule—staying up all night and sleeping through the day.

Joe parked on the street. "Just got word from Dupé he cleared this conversation with our subject," he said to her via the earbud. "This software must be top secret."

"I told you." She'd forced him to contact the West Coast Director to make sure Kyle didn't put up resistance to the questions Joe was about to hit him with.

As Joe got out of his vehicle, he scanned the area. She was sure he'd already noticed the unmarked car down the block, but she alerted him anyway. "The Marshal is twenty yards west. He'll be running your plates before you're in the front door."

Joe headed up the sidewalk and swung around to the side where stairs went to the second level. "Let me know if our friend makes a move to join us."

"Roger that.".

It felt good to be working with someone again, Joe specifically. During their FBI days, they'd rarely crossed paths, since he specialized in kidnappings and she was in counterterrorism.

But when she surfaced after each undercover op, the Bureau insisted she decompress in the office—i.e. sending her to a shrink to make sure her head was still on straight—and a couple of times, she'd assisted Joe's team with missing persons.

Unfortunately, she hated every minute of those cases, except when working directly with him. He could outthink most kidnappers in no time, and it was a thing of beauty to watch him in action.

Kyle answered the door. He and Joe exchanged pleasantries and Kyle informed him Dupé had already called granted him permission to discuss Operation Quiet Streets.

She heard the sounds of Joe following Kyle inside, kitchen sounds alerting her to the kid pulling something from the fridge, getting a glass from a cupboard.

"Energy drink?" Kyle asked.

"No thanks," Joe replied. "This shouldn't take long."

"Dupé said you're chasing a criminal and had questions about my program. Like, if it could help you catch him?"

Sam wasn't surprised the director hadn't shared details about Joe's target.

"Word is it's highly effective at pointing out terrorists before they even commit a crime. Could it do that with other criminals as well?"

"It's still in beta," Kyle said, but she could hear the pride in his voice, "but we've had a lot of success so far. The more data we retrieve, the better the predictive abilities get, so yeah, it's possible."

"I'm not sure I understand exactly how something like this works. I'm not a computer" – he stopped and Sam read his mind, automatically filling in the word *geek*— "expert, like you are, so you'll have to speak English, okay?"

"Sure, man. You're familiar with the basic sources to detect terrorist networks, right? Open source intelligence, terrorist websites, intelligence records, email, phone signals, that kind of thing?" Joe must have nodded because Kyle went on. "The U.S. considers preemptive attacks a legitimate strategy. My software takes those basic sources and goes farther. We call it Quiet Streets. You've probably heard of Quiet Skies?"

"The thing with the airlines?"

Shuffling, the clink of glass. "Similar, except mine is much more sophisticated." Again a note of pride. "That program specifically targets travelers who are not necessarily on watch-lists, or under investigation by any agency per se, but have flags in their personal history, or the places they're traveling are known terrorist hotspots."

"They're profiling unsuspecting Americans," Joe said. "Thousands are being subjected to targeted airport and in-flight surveillance by undercover Air Marshals."

She heard Kyle's return to the fridge, and he sounded

unfazed by Joe's disgust. "Your neighborhood is where the battle is these days, dude. I mean, people have a public life, a private life, and a *secret* life. The latter might include innocuous things like gambling, or something a lot more extreme such as planning a dirty bomb." The ice maker went off, fell silent, as he got a drink. "Even the people close to them may not realize their son or friend is unraveling."

"And your program does that how?"

A drawer rattled. "It narrows in on specific soft spot targets where there are large, unsecured crowds. Specific neighborhoods with a high-risk index." Excitement laced his voice. He probably didn't get to talk about his pride and joy that often. "I can cluster potential threats, using sociocultural, political, economic, and demographic factors. Hell, it even considers voting patterns."

"For what exactly?"

"All those factors enhance the predictive ability. I can identify those most likely, if they have the resources, to become suicide bombers or gunmen. The top one hundred subjects are sent to the QS team and they decide who to target with surveillance." Silverware clanked against a plate before he continued. "If a suspect moves to the top ten, undercover agents make friends with them, offer resources to see if they'll take the carrot. They gain more data on the subjects, which I add to the software's analytical database. It continues to refine the attack probability factors and spits out an accuracy number. If that percentage gets high enough, the UCs give the suspect enough rope to hang him- or herself."

Sam asked Joe to clarify, and he repeated her words. "So… quantitative and qualitative analysis helps you determine the odds of attack within a specific neighborhood by people who match a certain profile."

Kyle spoke with food in his mouth, but sounded happy Joe understood. "In laymen terms, yeah. It's partially based on data from the Naval Research Laboratory, result patterns, and predictors by some of our international partners, like Israel."

"Israel?" Sam asked, and Joe echoed the question.

"High amounts of terrorism in their history." Chewing noises. "Suicide bombers, in particular, focus on accessible crowds such as shopping centers, synagogues, and mosques. What I'm doing is taking the research they and the NRL did and adding my own spin." His smugness was obvious. "I can look for people who fit a parameter in a specific neighborhood with a defined background and a few other demographic and political variables." A finger snap. "Bam."

Tense silence hung, and Sam imagined Joe holding back his temper. "Once you find them, what happens?"

"I earmark them and send the info up the line to the QS team."

"You could be ruining people's lives with this." Sam heard the preachy tone in Joe's voice and swore under her breath. "You're predicting something they're gonna do before they do it. What about free will?"

Kyle made a soft grunt of dismissal. "Not my problem. The FBI and Homeland get to decide who they're going after. If their undercover agent gets in deep and thinks there's a high probability the subject is going through with an act, and my data backs it up, it's up to the big wigs to decide if they should take out the terrorist. All I'm doing is giving them a more detailed methodology for proof of principle. That's what they're looking for."

Nothing moved on the street. Sam made sure the Marshal was still in his car. It appeared he was on the phone, probably checking Joe's plate as suspected, and she made her way downstairs and out the back door of the empty building.

"Ask who has access," she said. "Specifically, who sees the analyses he comes up with."

In her ear, she heard Joe query Kyle, and the computer geek

recite what he'd already mentioned. "Look, all I do is send the flags on to my contact on the Quiet Streets team. They take it from there. I don't understand the inner workings of the gov."

"Who does?" Sam muttered, using the cover of a bus to cross the street and duck behind a series of older cars in the drive between Kyle's building and that of the neighbors'.

"But you know Director Dupé?" Joe asked.

The students, still sleeping off last night's drunk fest, had left cups and beer bottles on the assorted car hoods. The smell of stale beer hung in the air as she snuck behind that house and into Kyle's backyard.

"Only by his rep. Never talked to him personally."

The hedge was so overgrown, it perfectly hid the Marshal's view from the lower rear entryway. It had been sealed off from the downstairs and was probably only used in bad weather.

The steps creaked, nearly too narrow for Sam's boots, but no one seemed alerted to her presence and she stopped on the outside of the door at the top to make sure she wasn't about to walk into the kitchen where the two were having their conversation.

In her earbud, she heard Joe again. "Seems odd you don't send any of these directly to Dupé or even Dr. Walsh. He's head of the Domestic Terrorism Taskforce."

"I know who he is. I only send him and Dupé agent analyses."

Agents? Like an echo, she heard Joe's surprise. "They run this software on them?"

"Sure. Guess they want to catch any who might go to the dark side." Running water. "It happens, you know."

She could see Joe frowning but all she could think was, *bingo!* "Ask about local agents. Has he run a profile analysis on those working in San Diego?"

Joe repeated her question.

"Sure. That gal that set off the bomb at the parade. An agent on the QS team had me run an analysis on her—Rosenthal, I think her name is?—last year."

"Who?" she whispered.

The floor inside creaked and she heard the sounds of the men moving to another room. As she suspected, the back entrance was unlocked, and she slowly opened the door, cringing as the hinges squeaked.

"Who was the agent? Was it Walsh? Dupé?" Joe asked, "What did the analysis conclude?"

"All the requests come through them. Can't say anything definitive about the analysis. I don't look at the results—top secret stuff—but I'm guessing the percentage was high since she went rogue. They should have caught that, huh?"

There was the sound of clicking on computer keys. Sam stood in a tiny closet-like space that held a compact washer and dryer unit, some cleaning supplies on a shelf, and a hot water heater with an older bicycle haphazardly shoved against it. Two jackets hung on hooks. Dust and dirt clung to everything. The space smelled moldy.

Carefully, she maneuvered past the obstacles and found herself outside the kitchen. Slipping in, she could hear them elsewhere and peeked through to view a living room that had been turned into an office space.

Kyle sat at a desk filled with computer equipment and two large screens. Joe stood with his back to her, looking over the kid's shoulder at something on one of them.

Silently, Sam stuck a listening device behind a cheap pantry unit. The miniature camera went over the doorframe, facing Kyle's workspace. To his right was the entrance that led to the outside steps at the front of the duplex.

The kitchen smelled of cold pizza and looked like a scene from the movie *Twister*. Every surface was covered with dirty dishes and random items. The door of the older white fridge held flyers, notes, and pictures, all attached via magnets. Several held more than one thing.

Front and center, a large magnet with the motto *Dance like no one's watching, Encrypt like everyone is* held a used bar napkin with a woman's loopy handwriting on it. Under her name and number, she'd left the outline of red lips.

Hoping she hadn't picked up any roach hitchhikers—there were bound to be plenty here—Sam let herself out, quietly closing the door behind her and going downstairs on silent feet.

Kyle's apartment hadn't exactly been cool, but the heat and humidity hit her full in the face as she emerged outside. The info Kyle had produced pinged around in her brain.

He hadn't said it outright, but the data he relied on was about people repeating patterns, embracing their labels, whether cultural, political, or economic. People repeated patterns that got them into trouble sometimes, just like Jimmy T, who'd ended up on that top ten list of Kyle's.

She wanted to believe that this type of thing had only begun in an effort for the government to develop recommendations for heightened public awareness in certain areas. To keep explosions from happening thirty thousand feet in the air, or, like her bomber, from injuring innocent people at a well-attended parade celebration.

Kyle was right about one thing; terrorism was no longer something that happened elsewhere. The battlefield was an all-out war fought by citizens as well as soldiers.

As she drove away, she realized she needed a new plan. Her battle wasn't on the street, but in a boardroom somewhere.

Through the earbud, Joe snapped her back to the present. He'd said goodbye to Kyle and was headed to his car. "This is total bullshit. I'm all for protecting our country, but I can't believe they're moving on targets before they've even committed a crime."

She had no answer. When she'd agreed to go undercover to see if Jimmy T was indeed a strong probability to act on his beliefs and blow something up, she'd felt she was doing the right thing. Stopping terrorists before they could hurt innocent people was never wrong.

"Sam? Are you there?"

"I'm here." Her voice cracked. Knowing someone had run an analysis on her made her gut fire up.

"Where do you want to meet?" Joe asked. "We need to come up with a plan."

Did he believe she was innocent? She still wasn't sure.

While it pained her, for now, she couldn't risk putting him in any more danger. She needed time to think, to figure out where to go next.

Hopefully, not prison. "I'll be in touch."

Yanking the device off, she tossed it and the transponder out the window. Hearing the crack of it hitting the pavement and watching in the side mirror as it shattered into a thousand pieces seemed like a metaphor of her life.

6

---

*E*vening

Dusk. The humidity had lifted and now everything was dry, heat rising from the pavement in waves as the sun blasted away for its last few minutes above the skyline.

Joe drove slowly through a rundown neighborhood, the car's air conditioner on full blast. Jack-Jack hung his head out the passenger window.

Sam had left him when they'd gone to Kyle's, which surprised Joe, and she hadn't come back for him, which surprised him even more. He gripped the steering wheel tighter, thinking about strangling her if—*when*—he caught her for leaving him high and dry after the interview.

He'd had her in his grasp again and let her get away. Following her had been a bust and he'd ended up back at his place with the ragtag dog and a note telling him she'd planted a listening device and a camera in Kyle's.

God, she was good. Too good. He'd heard her enter that damned apartment and kept Kyle from picking up on it. He'd purposely positioned his back to the kitchen, blocking movement while the kid monitored his social media accounts during the interview.

Now, thanks to Sam breaking in, he had an illegal tap on the place. He wasn't sure what to do about it—be happy he could keep an eye on the geek, or worried if he did come up with anything pertinent to Sam's case, it wouldn't be admissible in court. Joe could lose his license.

His brothers would love that. He'd never hear the end of it.

Not that Cabe or Malachi were above bending the law on occasion, but they were very careful to cover their tracks. The Marshal keeping an eye on Kyle's would have evidence Joe had been there, and his fingerprints were all over both pieces of equipment, since they belonged to him.

Joe turned on a street in one of the worst sections. Definitely not a place most went after sundown. Abandoned buildings, an empty warehouse with plenty of broken windows, and a strong gang presence kept smart people away. Tonight, thanks to the heat, the streets were deserted. The area felt like a ghost town.

Volunteers all around the city were rounding up the homeless to get them in to air-conditioned places. More spread throughout the city, distributing fans to the elderly and those with low-incomes.

As Joe drove by the warehouse, his eagle eyes scanning for any movement or a car resembling the one he'd caught Sam driving to Kyle's, Jack-Jack suddenly stood. The dog looked right, tail wagging furiously, and let out a sharp bark.

Joe slowed more, craning to peer in the same direction. Jack-Jack appeared quite different than he had earlier, thanks to a groomer friend. Jack-Jack had put up a fight when Joe dropped him off, but Wymetta had managed to get him bathed, trimmed, and even provided a flea treatment.

"What is it, boy?"

Joe did a U-ey and started back the way they'd come. The

dog jumped into his lap, practically knocking his head into Joe's window.

As they came to a cross street, Joe took a chance and wheeled right. He wasn't sure where this one led, but he could see an old abandoned viaduct bridge a few blocks away.

Jack-Jack began to go crazy again, practically trying to jump out the window when Joe rolled it down. The dog barked loudly and fidgeted on his lap to the point Joe had to struggle to see around him.

"Okay, okay. I got it. Is this where she is?"

They crept down the street, partially because Joe was fighting to see around the dog's head, and also because if this *was* where Sam was hiding out, he didn't want to scare her away.

As they drew closer, he pulled to the curb. Before the car came to a complete stop, the dumb dog launched himself free and started down the sidewalk at an all-out run.

Joe didn't take time to roll up the windows, slamming the car into park and taking off after him. He hoped there wasn't anyone around, because if there was, he probably wouldn't have much car left when he returned.

The dog was fast, and before they'd gone a block, Joe was sweating hard. The bottom of the bridge came in to view, and Joe pulled up to catch his breath. What he saw made him do a mental fist pump.

In the sinking glow of light, he could just make out three figures in the distance, an assortment of lawn chairs near the edge of a swampy looking pool of water. Most likely the industry around here that had long ago died away had pumped run-off from their manufacturing into it.

As Jack-Jack barked furiously, running to greet the people, all three jumped to their feet, on alert. The one in the middle now had a flat brown hair color, totally nondescript, but he knew that sexy body and the exasperation coming off it, as she started toward him.

The other two—an older, skinny female, and a tall, younger guy—watched as she kneeled and embraced Jack-Jack first. The dog threw himself into her arms, and she scruffed his ears, allowing him to kiss her face, before standing and putting her hands on her hips.

By the time Joe was within earshot, the other two had joined Sam, one on each side of her in some weird solidarity. "That's far enough," she declared.

The older lady held a knife, the last vestiges of light bouncing off the blade. The guy, hardly more than a teenager, carried a baseball bat. Jack-Jack trotted toward Joe, wagging his tail and looking between him and the group.

"You forgot your dog," he told Sam.

"Told you, he's not mine. How did you find me?"

Joe pointed at Jack-Jack. "Like I said, *your* dog."

Sam's gaze fell to the mutt. "Traitor."

Jack-Jack wagged his tail, trotted in her direction and sat at her feet, looking up at her with adoration.

"I've got food and water in the car," Joe said to Sam's companions. Neither moved, although the woman licked her lips.

"Leave it on the sidewalk and we'll get it after you go," Sam instructed.

"How about I get it and bring it to you?" Joe argued. "Then you can tell me why you bugged that kid's house and left me responsible."

Sam muttered something to her friends and walked forward, lowering her voice. The two walked a few paces away, but kept an eye on her and Joe. "It will help with your investigation. We need to know who's contacting him or if there's anyone he's working for that he forgot to mention."

"Why him for this program?" Joe asked. "Why didn't Home-land use one of their own?"

Sam gave a shrug. "Asked myself that question a few times. I'm guessing he's developed more than one program for us—I mean, the government. He doesn't seem to have any problem with ethics, all he wants to do is code software. My under-standing is he's done a lot of beta testing for different organiza-tions, and think about it. In all honesty, he's fairly expendable. If anything goes wrong, he's technically not on the payroll. They can put all the blame on him, if need be, or simply get rid of him if he causes any issues. No one will be the wiser."

That was one of the things that had bothered him while pondering this kid's high intellect and lack of common sense. "Come home with me, Sam. Let's talk this thing through from the ground up, and get you out of this." He motioned around with his hands.

She glanced over her shoulder. "Hey, you two, it's okay. You can relax."

"You sure?" The young man tapped the end of the bat against his leg. "I'm happy to run him off for you."

The kid had balls, Joe had to give him that. He was under-weight, possibly a junkie, and even with the weapon, Joe could take him down in a flat second. But he kind of liked the idea that Sam had somebody, two somebodies, watching out for her.

Sam gave the kid a smile. "If I holler, you come with that bat raised."

Reluctantly, her two friends returned to the camp, the old woman throwing glares over her shoulder at Joe. He started toward Sam at the same time she moved, and they met in the middle. Jack-Jack nosed around at their feet, wagging and trying to get their attention.

Joe knelt and rubbed between his ears. "I swear, Sam, I'm on your side. I can't sleep knowing you're out here, exposed. Let go of your paranoia for a second and let me help you."

She bit her bottom lip and glanced around, nervously scanning the area. He couldn't imagine what it was like to be on the run all this time, to be afraid to show your face in public. She'd become the number one terrorist on the U.S. top ten list overnight.

She reached into a pocket and withdrew a crumpled piece of paper. Unfolding it, she read whatever was on it for a moment, then held it out to him. "Here is a list of suspects. I can tie each of them directly to the undercover operation and they possess the resources to pin the bombing on me. I don't understand the motivation behind it, but this is the only place I know to begin, now that I understand Kyle's program and the way they're using it."

He took the paper, noticing the dirt and creases. "Okay, let's go. We'll start on the list tonight."

A shake of her head. "I can't go with you."

"You don't trust me?"

Her eyes darted away. "I *do*, that's why I'm giving you the names. But I'm way too hot to stay with you. You're under surveillance, and the risk is too great."

Frustration sang in his veins, hotter than the day's heat on his skin. "Come for an hour, nothing more. Let me feed you. Take a shower—you stink. You can rest, then return here if you want. While you're doing that, I'll dive in to the list."

Her reluctant smile tugged at his heart. "You always did try to take care of me."

He desperately wanted to reach out and touch her. Grab her and give her a good hard shake. What the hell was wrong with her? "How about this? I'll get a hotel room. We'll order room service."

Jack-Jack whined at her. She turned her smile on him. "I really want to, Joe, I do."

But she wasn't going to. Maybe if he could just get her to the car, he could wear her down. "It's okay, I understand. Come get the food and water from my car, at least."

Maybe he'd simply kidnap her.

Her smile turned rueful. "Nice try."

It was like she could read his mind, and he chuckled without humor. "You gotta give me points for trying."

"Like I said earlier, I'll be in touch."

His phone buzzed and he started to ignore it, but she turned her back on him and walked toward the camp. Jack-Jack look confused, not sure whether to follow or stay with Joe. Joe used his fingers to motion him to go with Sam. The dog was smart. He did.

His caller ID read Roman Walsh. Damn.

"Cahill," he answered.

The director's next words made Joe's blood run cold, even in the heat. "Kyle Dunmire is dead."

Silence hung on the open line. Joe cursed. "You can't be serious. When did this happen? *How* did it happen?"

Sam was still close enough to eavesdrop and she pivoted sharply to look at him. Joe motioned her back and she slowly walked in his direction, brows furrowed.

"We're not sure about the details yet," Walsh told him, "but it's possible you were the last to see him alive."

The rest of Walsh words sounded muffled in Joe's ears, a dull ringing invading them. The director told him he'd call with further details as they came in, and Joe disconnected.

"What's wrong?" Sam asked.

Joe pocketed the phone, the implications of what happened screaming in his mind. "We have a big problem,"

"Bigger than the fact I'm a terrorist?"

"Sam." Things had gone from bad to worse. "Kyle is dead."

7

———

*S*am's legs trembled. She was already sweating, but a new wave—this one cold—washed through her. The bag of chips she'd scrounged for dinner threatened to come up. "Oh my god."

Joe took several steps toward her. It had to be getting close to eight-thirty/nine o'clock from the shadows falling around them. Her eyes played tricks on her in twilight and he appeared slightly blurry. "Medical examiner suspects food poisoning or allergic reaction. The kid was found in a pool of vomit, with sushi on the kitchen counter."

Her ears began to buzz. "What?"

Joe looked as unconvinced as she felt. "No official cause of death from the coroner until tomorrow. The Marshal saw no one coming or going after I left. Walsh wanted to know if the kid was okay last I saw him."

Acid rose into her throat. "Oh shit."

"Exactly." Joe took another step closer. "Kyle was involved in a highly classified project with you—my former lover—who is now considered a terrorist, at the center of it. And after I interviewed him, he's found dead."

He was too close. She knew she should move. He might try to overpower her and drag her off. She told her feet to step back, but they were anchored to the ground. "They got to him."

Joe didn't seem surprised by her train of thought. "You think the people who set you up killed Kyle?"

"Of course!" Why, she wasn't sure. He was an outsider, an innocent, wasn't he? She reached for something to keep her from falling into a pit of despair. "The camera, Joe! And the listening device. Maybe we caught the assassin."

Joe nodded, his gaze so intense it added to her lightheadedness. "The listening device wasn't transmitting earlier when I checked. Must be a dud. Come home and we'll review the camera footage together."

Home. He still thought of his place as their home, the one they'd shared together. Deep in her heart, she did, too. Being there this morning had brought dozens of happy memories rushing back. The thought of food, a shower, a bed—*Joe's bed* —filled her with such longing.

She glanced at his hands, one still holding his phone, and wished he'd wrap his arms around her, make this awful nightmare stop. "You believe me now?"

His pause was a heartbeat too long. "I believe there's more to this investigation than either of us understands. You're right, we may have caught the killer on video, *if* Kyle was intentionally murdered. Maybe he had an allergy to something in the sushi or it was bad. The only way to know is to examine that footage."

"Do you see why I installed the camera? It was the right thing to do."

"It may help us, yes." He was using his calm, friendly voice. Trying not to scare her. Did he realize just how badly frightened she was?

"I shouldn't have dragged you into this." The heat was so oppressive. Her stomach continued to rage, threatening to embarrass her, and her limbs felt like jelly. *Poor Kyle.* "I want your word you won't turn me in or try to get me to do it myself."

"If I planned to take you in, don't you think I would've done it already?"

The touch of cockiness aggravated her, but she preferred that over him handling her with kid gloves. She raised her chin in defiance. "Swear it."

He sighed and returned the phone to his pocket, held up his big hands in surrender. Hands that had caressed her body, supported her, provided a lifeline when she had none. "I swear. I have no plans to follow through with this bounty, and I know better than to try and talk you into doing something you don't want to. All I'm attempting at the moment is to figure out what the hell you've gotten yourself into."

Her breath hiccupped at the realization he truly was going to help her. Head swimming, she blinked away the vertigo. Before she landed flat on her ass, she bent down, acting as though she needed to say good-bye to Jack-Jack. The ground tilted and she nearly tipped over, even as she reached for him.

Jack-Jack braced his feet, steadying her. He licked her face and she clung to his neck, whispering in his ear, "Thank you. You're looking good by the way. If I can come back for you, I will."

He wagged his tail and licked her again, making her chuckle.

Joe gently took her elbow and helped her stand. "He's coming with us."

"You couldn't wait to get rid of him earlier. Now you wanna take him with us?"

"I have the feeling he isn't going to let you go anywhere without him again."

Sam withdrew from Joe's grip, even though his steadying solidness felt wonderful. "He's a good boy. Smart. You won't have any trouble with him, and I swear I won't leave him at your place again."

Jack-Jack barked his approval, and she knew by the way Joe nodded and started walking away he was giving her the dog as a concession. Knowing her the way he did, he believed she'd feel safer with Jack-Jack there, and he was right.

"Your choice," she told the mutt. She motioned at Hetty and Dec. "You can stay with them and I'll be glad to know you're keeping watch over our friends." A glance toward Joe's retreating back, and she noticed the tightness in his shoulders. It was taking everything in him not to look back to see if she was following. "Or you can go with me and that guy."

Jack-Jack barked and took off after Joe.

"I take back what I said about you being smart," she called after him. Facing the tiny camp, she waved at Hetty and Dec. "I'll return as soon as I can."

She'd intended to sneak off during the night anyway. Patterns, comfort zones...she'd already overstayed, gotten complacent and protective about these two. If someone *had* killed Kyle—she shuddered.

The horrifying notion Hetty and Dec could be in danger because of her made her knees weak again. No. She'd been careful. No one had followed her here. Leaving her backpack with them, she waved again and forced her feet to follow Joe.

He was waiting at the corner, scanning the area, always alert for trouble. There were no active streetlights in this section and the scenery was gray and shadowy. At night, the buildings looked like leftovers of a battle zone. With Jack-Jack trotting beside her, the two of them got in the car.

Joe turned the vehicle around and headed for the freeway. "Water's in the back."

She was dehydrated, and he knew it. Glancing over the seat, she saw a cooler. Jack-Jack was in her lap, front paws on the door and his head hanging out the window. She'd have to move him in order to twist around, but her limbs felt like heavy weights. Her head, too. She laid it against the headrest and closed her eyes. "I can't believe they killed him. Why would they do that?"

Joe didn't answer, seemingly intent on getting them out of this part of town. Or maybe he thought her theory was edged with too much conspiracy.

She dozed, and the next thing she knew, Jack-Jack's tail was beating her face and they were in a parking lot across from Joe's condo. Living close to the beach, even at this time of night, there was activity up and down the streets and on the distant boardwalk. Tourists and vacationers were heading in after a long day on the sand, or out to the nightclubs.

Joe handed her a bottle of water. "Drink up. You're going to need to use whatever covert operation you did this morning, since the Marshal is still here. Can you make it in on your own?"

She felt better after the nap and drank half the water before answering. "Of course."

The thought of trudging through the lot, past the condominium building attached to it, crossing the street and getting into Joe's without raising any suspicions actually sounded like more than she could handle at the moment. All this time on the run, and now the death of a somewhat innocent college student—quite possibly because of her—had worn her down to a very fine point. At any moment, she felt as if she might go postal, or dissolve into a bucket of tears. She wasn't sure which.

No tears. She could hear her dad's voice. He'd been tough on her over the years, but right now, she was glad he'd taught her to only use them when she needed to manipulate someone.

It sounded cold-hearted and cruel, but in undercover work, it had come in handy more than once. She could play the emotional woman when needed and get information or help.

The only time she cried for real was behind the bathroom door with the water running.

Show no weakness, Dad had always said. If you needed to let out emotion, go hit something. He'd given her a bat for that very purpose and there were many times when she'd taken it to her pillow. Once to her brother, Larson. He was three years older and a lot bigger, and even with their dad's training, it didn't take long for him to manhandle the weapon from her. He'd still ended up with a couple bruises, but nothing worse.

"Sam?"

Screwing the cap on the bottle, she patted Jack-Jack on his back, and nodded. "I'll be there in ten."

She let the dog out and he ran to a tiny two-by-two section of grass with a palm tree and peed on it. Her legs were more stable, but she still had to move slowly. Joe told her to be careful, and she closed the door.

Waiting until she found an opportune moment, she slipped in with a group of twenty-somethings dressed in party clothes ten minutes later to cross the street, then behind an Escalade parked near the side entrance of the building.

A couple walked by, probably returning from dinner and the woman caught sight of Jack-Jack. "Beautiful dog," she said to Sam as they headed inside.

Sam smiled and picked him up, following. "He's amazing. Very loving."

The woman was a little tipsy, but kept talking as they entered. "Do you live here? I didn't think we were allowed to have dogs."

"Just visiting a friend."

It was dangerous letting anyone see her who might be able to identify her, but she was too tired to care at the moment. Simply carrying on a fake conversation took all her willpower, but soon she was home.

He'd microwaved a burrito for her and had her favorite

salsa and a large glass of water waiting on the breakfast bar. She wanted to see that video, but the smell of the food was too much. Without a word, she hopped on the stool and started shoveling it down.

Joe left her alone, which was appreciated, and made sure Jack-Jack had a bowl of food. The dog ate it all and drank a matching bowl of water. When Sam finished her meal, she found both of them in Joe's office. He was scanning footage from Kyle's apartment and paused it until she pulled up a chair and settled beside him. Jack-Jack jumped in her lap and laid down.

Joe's face showed little emotion, but the eyes, that was her clue. He was tired, and worried, but relieved too. He scanned her face, seemed satisfied she was in better shape. "Ready?"

She inhaled deeply, feeling a contentment settle over her. For now, she was safe. She nodded.

His finger tapped a key and the video played. "Here we go."

8

———

"*H*ow did they discover the body?" Sam huddled over Jack-Jack, absentmindedly stroking him. Her voice was strained.

On screen, they watched Kyle answer a call that seemed to excite him. Whoever was on the other end made the kid light up like a Christmas tree. Joe silently cursed the dead listening device, but the camera's tiny microphone did catch a few things.

Even as Kyle spoke, he jumped up and began straightening the living room. "Of course! Now...fine."

Joe tinkered with the software, trying to enhance the acoustical feedback. "The kid is a TA and holds a study hall once a week. He didn't show up for the summer class he's in charge of at five. Phone calls were made, and eventually, Harris contacted the Marshal and sent him to check on Kyle. He was already dead."

The video continued as the conversation ended and Kyle hastily gathered dirty clothes lying around. He disappeared from view and a distant hissing noise could be heard. Joe fast-forwarded until he reappeared fifteen minutes later, carrying what looked like cologne and patting some on his cheeks. He'd obviously showered, his hair wet. His lips moved as if he were talking to himself.

Sam leaned in slightly, trying to hear what he was saying. "Is he getting ready for a date?"

Her body odor was something else, but regardless, Joe was relieved to have her next to him. At least for the moment, he didn't have to worry about her.

Jack-Jack lifted his head, seemed satisfied Joe and Sam weren't going anywhere, and went back to sleep.

Working through the footage until they found Kyle staring out the windows next to the front door, Joe speculated. "He's definitely waiting for someone."

"Someone he wanted to impress."

While the kid stood there, he fiddled with his phone. He began pacing, and seemed to be talking to an invisible person. From the little they could get from the camera's microphone, he was trying out various pick-up lines.

Joe internally grimaced at the kid's awkwardness.

Sam sighed. "That's just sad."

Kyle might've been a genius when it came to coding software, but he seemed completely petrified of whoever had invited themselves over.

"Wait. Stop." Sam pointed at the screen. "Back up."

Joe did, rewinding to a place where Kyle's head went from facing forward to whipping around to look behind him and into the kitchen, his brows furrowing. "Hello?"

Whoever appeared in his line of sight made those eyebrows jack straight up, as did the corners of his mouth. "How'd you get in there?" he asked the person off camera.

They couldn't hear a response, thanks to the defective listening device.

Sam shook her head in disgust as they continued to watch, the video feed picking up only the faintest noises once Kyle joined his companion. They heard laughing, and what sounded like a woman speaking.

Joe cranked up the volume, but the conversation was too indistinct. The tiny microphone on the camera was pointed in the wrong direction, at the living room. Was it too much to hope the couple moved into there, so they could see the visitor's face?

He had the damning feeling that wasn't going to happen. If this was their killer, she'd kept Kyle in the kitchen.

They heard the clank of plates and glasses. Walsh hadn't mentioned there was more than one of either found at the scene, but then the place had been a mess. There was the sound of low conversation and possibly eating and Joe continued to mentally urge them to move into camera range.

Minutes ticked by, both him and Sam listening closely. Things got quiet, and then...

Something heavy and solid hit the floor. There was a moan. As the seconds ticked by all sound ceased, and then a rhythmic *thud thud thud* came through the speakers.

Sam looked at Joe with wide eyes. "That was fast."

At least one of those awful lines Kyle had been practicing must have worked. He was going at it on the kitchen floor with his visitor. Joe turned the volume down a notch. "So, she came up the back way, didn't knock, and brought food. Apparently, she already had seduction on her mind."

"Or killing," Sam countered.

Kyle continued to make animalistic noises, but the woman stayed silent. They heard him finishing with a shouted curse, and Joe rolled his eyes. "Maybe she killed him just because he came first."

Sam smacked him. "Be serious. She entered that way to surprise him. Maybe she planned to sneak up on him and kill him, but why call and let him know she was coming over first?

She brought the food. I bet there's a toxin in it and that's what killed him."

Joe believed it was too much of a coincidence that Kyle had died today, but shit happened all the time. Maybe the kid really did have a bad reaction to the sushi, or there was some other culprit that had nothing to do with the woman. On the other hand, it didn't look good for her. "Who do you think she is?"

Kyle said something the microphone didn't catch and there was brief laughter from his sex partner. They heard bodies shuffling, before the sound cut out once more. Joe wanted to bang on the computer but that was pointless. A minute ticked by and then the sound wavered in with Kyle making a surprised cry. Soft murmuring from the woman, and the next thing they heard, retching noises.

Sam sat back, her face going steely. The retching continued for a full minute and then complete silence on the other end.

Joe held out hope perhaps the woman wanted something off the kid's computer. Like the software. *Come on*, he thought. *Head to the living room and let me see your face.*

She didn't. They watched until they were sure she'd left. The next person to show was the Marshal, breaking in through the front. From there on it was a steady stream of EMTs, the coroner, CSIs.

Joe flipped off the video and rubbed his jaw where three days' worth of growth was stubbly. "Who is she working for?"

"No idea." Sam sighed loudly, alerting Jack-Jack, who cracked his eyes open, ears perking. "We have to go back."

"To Kyle's? No way. It's too hot. The investigators have every-thing blocked off, and from all the activity, I'm guessing the entire neighborhood is watching the place. Even if the techs are gone, breaking in again would be stupid. Knowing Walsh, he's got even more eyes watching it now."

"There was a napkin on the refrigerator." Jack-Jack hopped down and shook himself. Sam stood and chewed on her thumbnail. "A woman gave him her name and number. How much you wanna bet she's our killer?"

"A napkin?"

"From a bar, like you'd put a drink on. He probably met her in one of the campus hangouts. We need to get in his kitchen and find it."

Joe rubbed a hand over his face. It had been a long day, and he had the feeling there were going to be a shit-ton more before this was over. "Okay, tell you what. I'll look for it. You stay here, take a shower."

She shook her head. "It's too dangerous. Our assassin could be watching as well. I don't want her anywhere near you, or…"

"What?"

She rubbed her temples and paced. "Whoever set me up must be behind this. Kyle died because of me. I want your help, but it's better if I do this alone. I can't put you in more danger."

She motioned at the dog and started for the back door.

Oh no. She wasn't getting away from him that easy.

He launched himself from the chair and caught her by the wrist. Not hard, just to stop her. "I want to get to the bottom of this as much as you do, and whether you stay or go, I'm in it. I'm not quitting. I'm not backing out, and I'm not letting you do this on your own."

"I have to. Don't you see? I have no idea who I'm up against and any connection to me will only land you in hot water."

"Let's take a minute and regroup. Seriously, Sam, you need a shower, if nothing else. While you clean up, I'll check in with the crime scene investigators and whoever I can think of, and see if anything has turned up in the past few hours."

She hesitated and it was all he needed. He could—would— convince her to stay. "They'll have pictures of the scene. I'm guessing everything they collected has been copied and sent to Harris and the SCVC Taskforce. I'll get looped in, and by the time you're done, we can scan them for that napkin and review the list of items they recovered. If it isn't in any of that, we'll do some recon on the apartment."

He saw the internal debate in her face. She was so damned stubborn, he held his breath.

She didn't try to pull out of his grasp, and instead moved toward him. Her head dropped to his chest. "God, I'm so tired."

Her surrender was so unexpected, he stayed frozen for several heartbeats. Then, slowly and carefully, he pulled her into an embrace. "You're living my worst nightmare," he admitted. "I can't imagine how tough this is. You're incredibly strong, and brave."

They stayed that way for long moments, and she seemed to melt ever so slightly. When she eventually raised her head, a sarcastic, faint smile danced on her lips. "You're right. I stink."

He brushed the bangs from her forehead and laid a friendly kiss there. "I'll get fresh towels."

He didn't want to let go, but he knew she was too skittish, even after admitting she needed him, so he gently released her and headed toward the hall closet. As she went into the bathroom and turned on the hot water, he fished around for her favorite set of towels and brought them to her.

He set them on the vanity. "I've missed you, you know."

She'd put the toilet lid down and sat on it, elbows on her knees, face in her hands. At his comment, she glanced up, and he saw the exhaustion and overwhelming challenges she faced in her eyes. "Yeah, well, don't get used to me being here. If they catch me, you'll never see me again."

A stark reality. One that made him even more determined to figure out what the hell was boing on. "I look at it this way," he countered, trying to alleviate the hardness in her face. "We either prove your innocent or we go on the run together."

She gave him a half-hearted smile and stood. "You're the last person I'd take with me."

He grinned. "Liar."

She laughed, and it was music to his ears. "You wouldn't survive three days on the streets."

"Wanna bet? I got a hundred that says you're wrong."

Her smile turned sardonic. "I hope I never have to test that theory."

Reluctantly, he left her, closing the door behind him. Jack-Jack positioned himself in front of it, as if guarding her.

Joe gave the dog a treat from the box he'd bought from Wymetta. "Good dog."

In the kitchen, he grabbed a beer from the fridge while he called Harris. It went to voicemail and he left a message, asking for an update as soon as he could get one.

Disconnecting, he heard his doorbell ring. Who the hell…?

Probably one of his brothers. Still, he picked up his Beretta and brought it with him, thankful the dog hadn't decided to go off.

"Shit." Through the peephole, he saw the last person on earth he wanted to find while harboring a fugitive in his bathroom.

There was no way he could ignore his unexpected visitor, though. All he could do was try to keep him from coming into the apartment.

Taking a second to collect his thoughts, he hurried to the bedroom and pulled the door closed. Luckily, Jack-Jack hadn't started barking at the sound of the doorbell – maybe the dog had never heard one since he'd been living on the streets. All Joe could hope was he didn't go off at someone else's voice.

At his front door, he undid the lock, and cracked it open.

Cooper Harris gave a nod. "Hey. I know it's late, but I was in the neighborhood when I got your message. I've got the preliminaries on Dunmire."

He held up a red file, and Joe mentally scrambled to figure out an excuse why he couldn't invite him in. He came up blank. "Perfect timing. I definitely want to see that tonight." He cracked the door wider but kept his body planted in the opening as he reached for the file. "I'd invite you in for a beer but I'm not feeling so great. I think the heat's getting to me."

Harris's eyes narrowed slightly. "Yeah, it's been a bitch, hasn't it? Heat index was a hundred and ten today."

They stood there, eyes locked, Joe trying to look sick, Harris trying to read his mind. At least that's how it felt.

The head of the SCVC wanted to discuss things in more detail, that was obvious, but he couldn't while standing in the hallway where anyone could overhear.

Joe tapped the file into his open palm. "Thanks again. Have a good night."

The big man didn't move nor say anything for another scrutinizing minute. "Let me know if you have questions." He took a step back. "Let's touch base tomorrow."

"Sounds good." Joe kept the door cracked as Harris left. Once he was sure he was gone, he closed and locked it, leaning back and letting out a long, relieved sigh.

He set the file on the counter along with his gun and went to the bedroom. Jack-Jack had left his post. Joe couldn't hear the shower.

Frowning, he crossed the bedroom and knocked lightly. "Sam? You okay?"

There was no answer. With a sinking feeling, Joe reached for the knob and found it locked. "Sam? Are you in there? Come on, open the door."

Useless. Gritting his teeth, he threw his shoulder into it, once, twice, and on the third, the lock gave, the door flying open and Joe toppling in.

The bathroom window was ajar, hot night air mingling with the steam from the shower.

Just when he'd finally gotten her to trust him, Sam was in the wind again.

9

The napkin was gone.

The computer, too.

Sam's stomach heaved when she saw the chalk outline. She paused out of respect. "I'm so sorry, Kyle."

She had no doubt he'd been murdered and she felt awful if her involvement—sending Joe to interview him—had caused any part in it. Whether the assassin, or the CSIs who'd swept the scene, had taken the napkin, she didn't know. Odds were on the woman.

Moving to the kitchen doorway, she reached for the camera mounted over the doorjamb. The backpack slung over her left shoulder snagged on a nail poking from the frame and she had to adjust it as she stood on tiptoes.

She considered scanning the rest of the apartment to look for Kyle's phone or anything else that might give her a clue to the woman's identity, but knew it'd probably be a pointless exercise and waste too much time.

She'd stolen the backpack—Joe's go-bag filled with supplies —from his closet when she'd heard Cooper Harris's voice.

She'd been looking through the clothes, snagging a pair of yoga pants she'd left behind and one of Joe's t-shirts.

The doorbell had startled her and she immediately felt panic grip her belly. All these weeks on the run had kept her constantly in flight mode, and she'd seized the bag before she'd even thought it through.

Jack-Jack had been a good boy and let her take him out the bathroom window, and thank goodness Joe lived on the first floor. She'd stolen a bike from the racks two blocks down at a different unit and they'd made their way through the dark city to Kyle's.

It was nearly midnight. The Marshal had been pulled, apparently, no one watching the place any longer. The neighbors were holding some kind of vigil, a cheer going up every once in a while for the dead USC student.

Sam wondered if any actually knew him and were distraught over his death, or they were simply looking for a reason to party.

Jack-Jack was in the tiny water heater room and she heard him bark softly, as if suggesting she hurry. Just to be thorough, she went through the living room and bounded upstairs to take a peek at Kyle's bed and bath.

Typical graduate student bachelor pad. Dirty clothes, used plates and glasses, a blanket hanging over one window as a shade. A quick inventory of drawers and the closet revealed nothing important and she hustled back downstairs using the tiny flashlight from Joe's bag to keep from turning on lights.

Avoiding the outline in the kitchen, she let herself and Jack-Jack out.

The group next door was drunkenly singing and she decided to take a chance. Wheeling toward them, Jack-Jack following, she stopped at the edge of the yard.

They had a small fire going in a round, metal fire pit, and it threw shadows across their faces.

One of the women noticed her and Sam waved. "Hey, there. Has anybody seen Kyle?" She threw a thumb over her shoulder pointing at the duplex.

The woman looked as though she were going to burst into tears. "Didn't you hear? Kyle died tonight."

Everyone was staring at her now, the singing fading. One of the guys stood and used his beer bottle to point at her. "You a friend?"

"You're kidding! He was going to tutor me for my comp sci class. I need to get up to speed before the new year starts next month. That's terrible. How did it happen?"

The woman walked toward her, wiping at her eyes. "They don't know for sure, but they think he had a reaction, like an allergy or something, to some bad takeout. What a way to go, huh?"

Jack-Jack moved in front of Sam, protective, and she petted him to let him know it was okay. "How awful. I didn't know him well, but he seemed like a super genius or something."

The woman nodded. "He wasn't exactly a social butterfly, but once in a while, we'd see each other in passing and he always made me laugh."

"He didn't seem overly social to me either," she said. "That's why I was excited when he agreed to tutor me. I was supposed to catch up with him at a study group earlier, but I couldn't make it. He told me to come by after I got off work. He said there was somebody else coming by, too. Did you see anyone? Not to be crass, but maybe she could help me?"

The guy who'd spoken handed her a beer. "Kyle didn't have many friends, and that gal he was seeing was no computer expert. I think you're out of luck."

"You know her?"

He threw an arm around the crying woman, but she was the one who answered. "We only saw her once or twice. It was pretty surprising, him having a girlfriend. I'm not really sure that's what she was."

Sam pretended to take a swig, and shook her head. "Damn. Guess it's back to the drawing board for me. Did you catch her name, by chance? Maybe she knows some of Kyle's computer friends and can point me in the right direction for another tutor?"

If the two of them thought it weird she was more interested in a tutor than Kyle's death, they didn't show it. The woman shook her head. "No idea. You might check with the department head, though. Kyle met her at a pool party put on by the guy. What's his name?"

A shrug from her partner. "Not my area."

"I guess it was a pretty big deal," she added. "Catered food, open bar, the works. Kyle was super nervous, but he thought the networking would be a good idea."

Sam nodded. "Guess he was right if that's where he met his girlfriend."

The guy finished his bottle, and swayed slightly on his feet. "She brought him home in a cab. Kyle was too drunk to drive."

"So you guys saw her?"

"From a distance," the guy replied, his forehead crinkling as if he was now beginning to wonder about all the questions. "She helped Kyle up to his apartment."

He kissed the woman on her cheek and went to get another beer. His girlfriend, nose red, crossed her arms and looked wistfully up at Kyle's. "He was happy, you know? That's what really sucks about the whole thing. She was probably his first girlfriend, like, ever. And I know he was about done with his master's. There were a bunch of different firms recruiting him to go to work for them."

She looked back at Sam with her sad, teary eyes. "*Carpe diem*, huh? You just never know."

"Can you tell me what she looked like?" Sam asked. "I think I might know who she is."

"She had real dark hair, and blunt bangs across her forehead. She wore expensive outfits. Taller than you, but thinner. I mean, she reminded me of a model you'd see in *Vogue* or something. Very exotic looking."

Could be a disguise. "Thanks." She handed the beer back. "Enjoy the rest of your summer."

"I didn't get your name," the gal said.

Sam adjusted the cap on her head and noticed a familiar car pulling up to the curb. Jack-Jack started wagging his stubby little tail, his ears perked, as he realized who it was. *Damn.*

"See you around campus," Sam said, wondering if she could escape Joe.

Probably not.

Joe had the window down and made a whistling sound. Jack-Jack ran for the car. "Throw your bike in the back," he called to her.

"Damn. Who is that?" the woman asked.

Joe unfolded himself and flipped the trunk up, staring at Sam with challenge in his eyes. He greeted the dog like they were long, lost friends before straightening with that look once more directed at Sam.

"He's hot," the woman said, and Sam could hear the lust in her voice.

He sure is.

She had a decision to make. Either believe Joe hadn't known Harris was going to show, or he'd called the man while she was in the shower and sold her out.

Her heart knew the truth, even though her paranoid brain insisted she couldn't trust anyone. She could almost hear her dad's voice drilling it into her brain—*trust is weakness.* Like love, it put a chink in your armor and left you open to betrayal.

She had to give Joe credit, he didn't move, didn't say

anything to cajole her into the car. He simply stood there, thumbs hooked in his pockets, daring her to put her life in his hands.

The din of the party faded and Sam stared back.

Jack-Jack returned to her, wagging his tail and panting. His goofy little face looked like he was smiling.

Joe, all muscles and five-o'clock shadow, called, "Your dog trusts me."

The unsaid conclusion hung in the air. *You should, too.*

There was no way he'd turned her in. She knew it down to her bones, but there was a part of her that still wanted to play hard to get, keep him on his toes.

Their relationship had always been a push-pull romance. Both nudging, poking, and prodding, always trying to gain the upper hand to keep the other person off guard a little bit. They were head strong, intense, and dedicated. To their jobs and each other. Usually, it was all in fun, but sometimes...

Sam wished she'd drank the beer. She wanted to go to Joe and let him put his arms around her. Allow him to beat back this nightmare and make it okay.

Trust. Love. *Weakness.*

Joe always told her love didn't make you weak. It made you strong.

Maybe he was right.

She patted Jack-Jack's furry head and started rolling the bike to the car.

10

***

"Where are we going?" Sam adjusted the seat belt. "You can't take me to your place. Too dangerous."

Joe still couldn't believe he'd gotten her in the car and allowed himself to take a deep breath. Her tired face was pale in the lights of the oncoming traffic, Jack-Jack lying in her lap, half-asleep. "North."

She shot him an impatient look. "Kind of figured that." She pointed at the sign on I-5 announcing Delmar was the next turnoff.

He eased his tight grip on the steering wheel. His pulse was still racing, and he commanded it to slow. Sam was with him. He could protect her, and he meant to do it right. "Somewhere safe."

A soft snort. "A safe place doesn't exist for me. You shouldn't be doing this. I never should've gotten you involved."

"They hired me to hunt you down. I already was."

The dark highway zoomed by under the tires. Jack-Jack shifted, turning around several times before lying back down with a huff. Absentmindedly, Sam stroked the dog's ears, staring out the window at the passing landscape.

"Okay, spill," Joe said. "What did you find out at Kyle's?"

"He supposedly met a woman at a Fourth of July pool party put on by the head of the computer science department. She brought him home in a cab. The gal I was talking to said she was exotic looking with dark hair and bangs. Taller than me and thinner. Could be our killer, but I have no proof of that." She stopped petting the dog. "Why would someone do this? Do you think it's my fault? Did they kill Kyle because of me?"

The anguish in her voice made his grip tighten once more. "We don't know that. You're jumping to conclusions, assuming she killed him. Maybe he truly had a bad reaction to the food."

Even to his own ears, the words sounded dubious. Kyle had been part of a top-secret, high-level government program, and Sam had mentioned how disposable he was to them.

Focusing on Kyle wasn't going to help anyone at the moment. Right now, he wanted and needed to focus on Sam.

"I know I have a reputation of being a conspiracy theorist," she said, "but this smacks of the conspiracy surrounding whoever set me up. I can't believe after the success of Kyle's program, they'd take him out, though. Whoever this woman is, she fits the profile of an assassin."

Joe passed a handful of mile markers before he said anything further, letting that soak in. Professional assassins weren't his area of expertise, but it seemed like overkill for a guy like the computer geek. "Tell me about your bomber."

"Why?"

"We need to start at the beginning."

She resumed scratching Jack-Jack's head and seemed to gather her thoughts. "Jimmy T was his name. T for Talbot. He was an All-American kid with parents who made him into a white nationalist. Strawberry-blond hair, goofy smile, whacked out ideas about taking back America."

This was good. Keep her mind off Kyle and his death and put that highly intelligent brain of hers to work on the bigger problem. "And why were you assigned to him?"

"Remember the Aztec Sports Arena bombing last year?"

"Of course. You identified that Kunez guy who tried to blow up first responders at the training. How could I forget? That's what started Alison's slide into hell."

The reference earned him a wry smile. Alison Kendrick had been Sam's boss. Sam had flagged Kunez as a potential terrorist and pushed it up the line. Following protocol, Alison should've notified Walsh's taskforce to analyze him and decide whether to put him on the watchlist or not.

The air conditioning had nothing on the chill in Sam's voice. "Alison did it to herself. She had an alternative agenda, and her failure to notify the Domestic Terrorism Taskforce about Kunez nearly cost dozens and dozens of lives. I still wish I could punch her out for that."

After Kunez had been identified as the bomber, Sam had contacted Walsh about her report. He'd claimed never to have received it. When questioned, Alison claimed Sam never filed it or brought it to her attention.

"You know how after that Dupé and Walsh got a hard-on for figuring out who Kunez was involved with? He wouldn't give up his brothers, but after they ran him through Kyle's software, he came back with an eighty-three percent likelihood of committing a terrorist act." She wiped her face with a hand. "That put our taskforce on the bandwagon for discovering if his closest family and friends might do the same."

Joe hadn't been around for all of that, having left the FBI by then, mostly thanks to Alison and her secret obsession with him. He and Sam had been together for three years at that point and he assumed he'd be with her for the rest of his life. Alison had other ideas.

Jack-Jack seemed to pick up on Sam's distress, opening his

eyes and raising his head to look at her. She scratched under his chin. "I flagged Jimmy T and we put him in Kyle's software. Seventy-nine percent. That's when they sent me undercover to recruit him."

She used the word loosely, its meaning far weightier. She'd been sent undercover to see if she could get Jimmy T to take his beliefs to a level where he committed a crime.

"You know the incident with Alison, especially her termination because of you, suggests strong motivation to frame you for something along this line."

Sam rubbed her forehead. After the fallout, Dupé had offered Sam Alison's job. She'd refused, wanting to stay in the field. "She doesn't have access to any of this anymore, though," Sam argued. "Her termination severed the access to databases, contacts, pretty much everything."

He didn't really want to think about that bitch, and the destruction she'd wrought on their relationship, as well as turning Sam into such a hardcore agent that nothing came before her job. "As conniving as she is, I believe she could do just about anything."

Sam was assigned to be at the Aztec Sports Arena that day for training. Through the grapevine, she'd heard Harris had been eyeballing her to join his taskforce, and she'd been excited about letting him see what she could do. Unfortunately, Alison had other plans, ruining Sam's by sending her to serve a warrant.

"The description of Kyle's girlfriend doesn't fit Alison either," Sam said, sounding disappointed. "Alison, with her fair hair and generous curves, is about as far from an *exotic* model as you can get." She toyed with the air vent. "Our assassin is good. I need to contact the comp sci department head and ask about that party, see if I can get more information on who our mystery woman is."

"*If* Kyle was murdered."

That earned another hard look. "There should be DNA, especially since they had sex. You need to make sure they do an autopsy and check specifically for that."

A sign let him know the turn for Carlsbad was a few miles ahead. "How exactly do you want me to do that? We illegally bugged Kyle's, and in actuality, caught nothing but the fact someone came to visit him. Yes, it sounded like they were indulging in some fun, and maybe she left DNA behind, but I need to approach that fact-finding mission carefully."

She fell silent, leaning on the headrest and closing her eyes. For once, he was surprised she didn't argue.

Sam slept until he pulled into the drive. Instantly alert, she sat up, disturbing Jack-Jack, who stood abruptly and shook himself, hair flying.

"You're okay," Joe said. "I didn't take you to jail."

"Where are we?"

In the dead of night, no one was near, and this place was never a bevy of activity for the most part. "Home, for now."

As they exited the car, Jack-Jack got down and started sniffing. Joe extracted his go-bag from the backseat and tossed it at Sam. He drew out a suitcase and two bags of groceries, hauling them up the front steps and plopping them by the door.

"Is this where you keep your mistress?" Sam teased.

At least she was getting the sarcasm back. "Yeah, you know me, always plenty of women hanging around." The opposite was true. He hadn't even looked at another woman since Sam had entered his life.

Maybe he should get a dog. At least then he'd have some company.

He let them in, flipped on the lights, and whistled. Jack-Jack relieved himself against one of the bushes before scrambling up the stairs. Joe reset the security alarm and allowed himself two seconds to release the pent-up tension between his shoulder blades.

She's safe.

The shades were drawn. Sam studied the place, taking inventory. Knowing her, she was logging all the entry and exit points. He offered a tour through the open living and dining rooms, to the rear of the place that contained the kitchen. While he put the groceries in the fridge, she surveyed the contents of the cabinets.

She pulled out tequila and two glasses. "I don't know about you, but I could use a drink."

As she washed her hands, he poured each of them a finger or two. After this day, a stiff one sounded good to him, too.

It was her favorite brand and she lazily accepted the glass he handed her and clinked it against his. "Thank you."

They both downed the shots and he set his glass on the table. "For the tequila?"

"For everything."

In the soft overhead kitchen light, he saw the depth of her exhaustion. Not just physically, but mentally and emotionally. "I want you to stay out of San Diego for the time being and let me handle the investigation."

She opened her mouth as if to argue, then snapped it shut. She poured herself another shot. Downed it. Studied him.

He went to a cabinet and removed a bowl, filled it with water and set it on the floor for Jack-Jack. The dog immediately helped himself and looked around. "Sorry boy. Left it in the car." As he went past Sam, he said, "Be right back. Make yourself at home."

She touched his arm and stopped him. "You don't have to do this, you know?"

Instinctively, he leaned over and kissed her temple. "Of course I do."

Outside, he grabbed the bag of dog food and a box of treats from the trunk. If Sam was going down in flames, he guessed he was as well.

Caleb and Malachi were gonna be so pissed when they found out. All he could do was find the proof he needed to clear Sam's name, or cut his ties with them before the shit really hit the fan.

Back inside, he filled the bowl and watched with satisfaction as the dog attacked the food. Sam had disappeared and he walked through the house following the lights she'd flipped on, discovering her in the large bedroom. She stood in front of the open closet doors lining the short hall between the bedroom and bathroom. "What is this?"

"What does it look like?"

She turned to face him. "An armory."

He shrugged. "I enjoy my toys."

"Are you planning for the apocalypse?"

He leaned on the doorframe and motioned at the closet opposite her. "You should be able to find stuff in there to wear and plenty of items to disguise yourself the next time I allow you to leave this house."

She kept an eye on him as she did a one-eighty, opening the other bi-fold doors. "When you *allow* me?"

He grinned, and she shook her head slightly, before examining the contents of the other closet. Once again, she appeared quite surprised. "Tell me you haven't embraced life as a drag queen."

"It's all for my mistress."

When she looked at him, he winked.

She fingered a row of the clothes, examined the shelf of shoes. "Wigs? Jewelry? Is she in witness protection?"

"Actually, there are times when I'm hunting a bail jumper that it comes in handy."

"I knew it. You're all about drag."

He was definitely not, but he couldn't tell her the truth. Not yet. More fun to go along with the teasing. Mistresses, drag queens...it was nicer than conspiracy theories and dead college students. "I might use some of this on occasion in the field. You'd be surprised how criminals let down their guard when they see a pretty woman coming at them."

Her mouth hung open for a second. Then she narrowed her eyes. "You've never dressed like a woman in your life. But nice try."

He boosted off the doorframe, took her hand, and led her to the bathroom. Smiling to himself, he waved a hand like a magician at the contents of the linen closet. "Makeup, falsies, and other items to assist changing your look."

"Falsies? Do you even know what that means?"

He did, but he played dumb. "Fake eyelashes?"

She rolled her eyes. "Seriously, whose house is this?"

Back in January, before things had gone topsy-turvy, he'd dreamed it would be theirs one day. "Just a safe house."

"You and your brothers run a bail bonds company. What do you need this for?"

"We have interests on the side."

That silenced her, and he left her standing there to keep thinking. Sam loved a good puzzle, and he intended to keep her guessing.

Returning to the kitchen, he gathered the ingredients to make a sandwich. He was finishing when she joined him. She filled a glass with ice and water this time and savored a long drink as she sat at the small kitchen table. "This feels like the Taj Mahal after the way I've been living."

"I'll bring more supplies to your friends tomorrow," he assured her. Slicing the sandwich in half, he placed a section on a plate for her. He stuffed the end of his half in his mouth.

Jack-Jack had been busy sniffing the house, and was currently rolling on the couch in the living room with wanton abandon. For the first time in days, Joe felt...happy.

If this all went to hell, he was going to be very *un*happy, and the likelihood of that was strong. This was without a doubt the most high-risk situation he'd ever found himself in, and he'd been in plenty.

Sitting across from Sam, he saw the tiniest amount of ease in her face, and that made every bit of risk worth it.

She attacked the food with as much abandon as Jack-Jack had the couch. Her cheeks rounded and she held a hand to her lips as she tried to speak. "Oh my god, a turkey sandwich has never tasted better."

They ate in silence, a familiarity wrapping itself around him. For a heartbeat, Joe imagined what it'd be like if they'd gotten married and moved here as he'd planned. How they might sit here, sharing a meal, while their mutt got dog hair on the sofa. It made him smile.

He allowed the dream to live while they finished their meal.

And then it got more interesting when Sam leaned over and kissed him.

11

———

$\mathcal{C}$*arlsbad*

Cooper Harris sank further into his sofa, staring vacantly at his non-working fireplace. He toyed with the half-drank beer in his right hand and contemplated a theory that'd been niggling at his brain all day.

"What are you thinking, boss?" Ronni sat in Cooper's favorite chair, staring at the coffee table with an expression similar to his.

He needed to get that fireplace fixed before fall came. Sure as hell didn't need it right now, but before he could blink, the nights would start getting chilly and Celina would want to use it so she could cuddle up next to him with a glass of wine before bed.

Cooper scrubbed a hand over his face. "We've been assigned a no-win investigation."

Celina trudged in, tossed a teething ring on the table and flopped down beside him. Her hair was tangled, eyes rimmed red. "Another one bites the dust," she said, pointing toward the teething ring.

Their daughter, Via, was ahead on the growth charts

according to her pediatrician and all the books Celina read, except in one area—baby teeth. She still had at least four trying to come in, and apparently, they'd decided to do it at the same time.

Cooper could run on little sleep, unlike Celina, who was similar to a cat and needed her beauty rest. She could crash for twelve hours if she wanted to. With this latest round of teething, however, Cooper found himself at the tipping point. It was one in the morning and he prayed Via would sleep the rest of the night, so both of them could sack out as well.

Ronni sat forward, elbows on her knees. She'd taken a friend at the Bureau to lunch to do a little digging on Samantha Rosenthal. "Connie said Rosenthal was focused on what she called 'the web' between all of these cases. Not the specific perpetrators or their allegiance to the various groups they were associated with, but something a little less tangible."

Celina slouched into the cushions and closed her eyes, kicking her feet up. Her toenails were a bright orange. "What does that mean? The web?"

Ronni yawned. "There may be connections between all the bombings in the past year, but I can't figure out what it is. Rosenthal's IQ is above mine, so she must've seen something that's invisible to the rest of us, because none of her superiors took it seriously, according to my friend."

Connie, a department secretary, had typed up various notes for Rosenthal and sat in on at least one meeting where the agent had broached her web theory about a collection of six different bombings since the Aztec Sports Arena.

"Okay," Cooper said, "but our job isn't to figure out her theory, only to bring her in."

"You don't really think her ex is going to do that?" Celina cracked one eye open to glance at him. "Imagine if the situation involved you and me. You'd never bring me in. If anything, you'd help me escape the country."

She was right. "You and I wouldn't be in this situation because you'd never mastermind a terrorist plot to blow up a bomb at an Independence Day parade," he countered. "On the other hand, if you *did* do something completely out of character like that, I'd probably get you across the border and run away with you, even if you were my ex."

She opened the other eye and smiled. That smile was worth everything. "So why do you all believe Joe Cahill is seriously trying to find Samantha and bring her in?"

"They weren't a couple anymore," Ronni said. "He proposed and she not only said no, she moved out."

Celina pushed herself upright. "Is there anything in her background that suggests she would commit such a horrible crime?"

She and Ronni stared at each other before Ronni turned her dark eyes on Cooper. "Agent Rosenthal is squeaky clean—or was until this."

Cooper tried not to sigh too loudly. These two created more havoc in his life than he cared for. He'd rather stay up every night until hell froze over with Via than dive into rabbit holes with Celina and her former partner. Together they were a force of nature on steroids.

"Before you go down that road, let me remind you again—the taskforce is assigned this case in order to assist Cahill in locating and bringing a fugitive to justice. We're not determining guilt. They already have proof against her."

Both women stared at him as if he were the devil. Celina clasped her hands. "You're using Joe as bait."

Cooper nodded. "He's the one person, according to Dupé and Walsh, she'll run to."

Ronni shook her head. "She'll see that coming a mile away. I'm no genius, and even I'd see that ambush."

Celina nodded. "Me, too. Dupé and Walsh are good at their

jobs, but they don't understand women. Especially those who are more intelligent than they are."

There was no winning an argument with them, and Cooper sucked on his beer to keep from engaging.

Celina spoke to Ronni again. "What do you think this web with the terrorists has to do with any of it?"

"What if Rosenthal stumbled onto something someone didn't want her to figure out?"

Celina seemed to really be coming to life now, her earlier sleep deprivation shoved aside. She leaned forward, mirroring Ronni's posture. "You think she found a link between the bombers that someone inside the Bureau didn't want her to?"

Ronni studied the cold fireplace, looking doubtful. "I just think there's more to this than meets the eye. This woman was brought up by two CIA operatives. Even once her mom left the field and had her, she was part of a counterterrorism analyst group inside Langley. Both spies were hailed as heroes. When they left the east and came here, they continued to consult for the CIA and NSA. Samantha also appears to have been an exceedingly good agent. What would make her snap and turn into a terrorist mastermind?"

"That's for the profilers to decide," Cooper replied. "It can take ten years to mold a terrorist or ten minutes. There was drama and scandal surrounding her and her boss last year. She got the woman fired. She may be a genius, but she could also have a few screws loose."

"Connie said there was misconduct between Alison Kendrick and Cahill. It's one of the reasons he left the Bureau."

Celina's brows shot up and disgust laced her tone. "He had an affair with her boss?"

"No. From what I understand, Kendrick wanted to but Cahill had no interest in her. He never filed formal charges, but the scuttlebutt is she made regular passes at him. Connie said he should have filed sexual discrimination charges, it was that bad. And everyone knew he was totally head over badge for Sam."

Cooper felt like he'd landed in a soap opera.

Celina tapped her fingers on the coffee table. "This happened while he was in a relationship with Samantha?"

Ronni nodded.

"People get crazy when love and sex are involved," Cooper said absentmindedly. "Maybe that's why Rosenthal snapped."

"I don't think so." Ronni stood and stretched. "I verified with Roman that Sam was offered Alison's position when she was terminated, but Sam turned it down. If she'd been after revenge, don't you think she would've taken it to rub it in her ex-boss's face?"

"Not if she was masterminding a terrorist plot," he countered.

Celina looked at him as if he were stupid. "Are you kidding me? That'd be the perfect position if she was."

He thought about it for a long moment and conceded. "You're probably right."

"I'm always right, and your taskforce needs to do a lot more digging into this terrorist plot. Sounds like there might be some plotting against Sam."

He was afraid she was going to say that. "You're suggesting someone in the Bureau set her up? If we stick our nose in that, we could end up in a world of hurt. I'm the first to weed out bad apples, but I can't put my taskforce on the line when we have nothing more than theories."

Ronni set hands to hips and stared at the coffee table again. "I want to figure out what Samantha found that linked the recent terrorist bombings here in California together."

"I want to know more about her and Cahill's relationship," Celina said. She looked at Cooper. "You should invite him over. Dinner tomorrow night?"

Ahh, shit. Cooper dropped his feet, set his bottle down, and slowly rose. "I'll think about it. I need to sleep on all of this."

Celina bounced up, acting as though she'd already had her twelve hours and was ready to go. She clapped her hands together. "Perfect. We're on it."

She moved around and hugged Ronni, before showing her to the door. "Drive safe and be here tomorrow for dinner."

Ronni waved at Cooper. "See you at the office, boss."

Once she was gone, he dumped the rest of the beer and rinsed the bottle before throwing it in the recycle bin. Celina followed him down the hallway, half-whispering so as not to wake Via. "Don't tell Roman or Victor about any of this yet, okay?"

Inside their bedroom, he pulled her close and shut the door behind them. Looking into her eyes, he placed his hands gently on her hips. "I don't need to remind you that you're not part of my taskforce anymore, do I?"

She went on tiptoes, throwing her arms around his neck. Her kiss was hot and deep. "I'll always be part of it," she whispered against his lips. "And regardless of your official assignment, you know there's something fishy about this whole situation. I can help figure it out."

God, he loved her. "Let's get some sleep, Mrs. Harris."

She pressed herself more firmly against him. "In a minute," she said, then started shedding her clothes.

12

———

Sam meant for the kiss to be a thank you. Like the previous day's had been.

Her body, however, had other ideas.

Joe's lips were warm and inviting. He tasted of tequila and the mustard on his sandwich.

Everything about him was safe, familiar, welcoming, and although he was holding up both hands as though she were pointing a gun at him, she knew it was only because he didn't want her to stop. If he touched her, if he deepened the kiss, he might frighten her away.

She was kissing a hero. A man who put everything on the line for her, not just this time, but previously as well.

She continued to lean across the table, her hands on his shoulders, her lips parted, encouraging his to do the same.

Maybe it was the liquor warming her veins, or simply a cog in her brain slipping. She was entitled, wasn't she? After her life had gone to hell, and spending all this time on the streets with nothing, the whole world thinking she was a terrorist, she deserved this respite. This moment of feeling safe and loved.

"Sam...?" Joe's voice, the hesitation in his eyes, made her

blink. He wanted confirmation she knew what she was doing. That this was what she really wanted.

Clarifying that she did, she kissed him hard and deep again.

Joe finally responded, grabbing her by the back of the neck and locking his lips on hers. Demanding, greedy. Like a starving man, he devoured her mouth, his tongue diving inside and forcing her lips to open even more.

He'd done so much for her, and now he'd brought her here, agreeing to help her uncover the truth. She owed him everything and she tried to convey it by matching his fervor.

Ever so slowly, she sucked in his bottom lip and ran her tongue across it. His sharp intake of breath told her he was still as sensitive to her as he'd always been. It was a rush knowing she had this kind of power over him. She hoped she was the only woman who ever had.

She knew there hadn't been anyone since her. Not that she'd been stalking him or anything, but she'd kept tabs on him all these months. She'd known even before she left on New Year's Day he was the only man who would ever hold her heart, but she'd hoped he would eventually move on and find some-one...normal. A woman who'd make him happy.

But secretly, underneath it all, she'd actually hoped he'd never be with anyone but her.

His hands skimmed her upper arms and he disengaged, setting her back an inch or so. "You don't have to do that," he said.

She felt lightheaded, and tried to convince herself it was simply the alcohol. "Do what?"

"Act like you owe me something."

It was a splash of cold water in her face. "You think I'm seducing you because I feel like I owe you?"

"I have to admit, it's not your style, but I just want to be clear."

She knew she should be insulted, but all she could was

laugh. It was so like Joe to call her on her bullshit. "Initially, I kissed you to say thank you, that's true. But it turned in to more."

He grinned. "Of course, it did. No one can resist my charm, especially you. I appreciate the kiss, don't get me wrong, and if you ever want to resume our relationship,"—he pointed both thumbs upwards—"I could easily be persuaded to. I'm all yours. But there are conditions."

She sat back and picked up the last of her sandwich. "What kind?"

"You kiss me like that again, and the wedding is back on. I don't care if I have to become a caveman and sling you over my shoulder, you're mine from that point on, and I'm never letting you go again."

"Is that it?"

A spark of the old Joe surfaced. "That's just the beginning."

She'd missed this. Him. But her heart was too fragile right now to discuss their relationship. The past was over, and she had no future with him. "I'll take that under consideration."

Under his watchful eyes, she polished off the food. "The people who were hurt in the bombing, are they all okay?"

He looked at her lips for a second, as if regretting the fact he'd rather resume the kiss, but nodded. "Most had minor injuries. Three were more serious, but they're all out of the hospital and on the mend."

She shoved the plate aside. "It could've been much, much worse."

He worked on his half, nodding. "It's been three and a half weeks and your trail has gone cold. Maybe whoever killed Kyle was looking for a way to put you in the spotlight again. Make certain people wonder if you were involved."

Sam's stomach flipped. "You're right."

"As long as we're working on conspiracy theories, seems like that would fit."

Her brain was too tired, and she really wanted a peaceful night of rest. "Have they leaked it to the press?"

Joe checked his phone, and after a minute of searching, clicked off. "Nothing yet."

She got up to head to the sink and as she was going by the table, he grabbed her wrist. Not hard or demanding, just making her pause. He took the plate from her hand and set it on the table. "I'm glad you're here." The corner of his mouth quirked. "I appreciate the kiss, too. If you have the need to thank me again, feel free."

Surprisingly, she laughed. "I have no idea why you're doing this, helping me, I mean."

"Maybe it's because I believe in you. I always have."

"They're using you, you know."

He shifted in the seat, drawing her in to stand between his knees. His beautiful blue eyes stared up at her, and she felt the old tug at her heart. "I'm the one who suggested it."

The world tilted. "You *volunteered* to apprehend me?"

"It was only a matter of time until they asked me to act as a lure. I figured I might as well offer my superior skills and abilities."

"You are so full of yourself."

"So are you. Did you really think you could go on the run by yourself, and still prove your innocence with no one helping you?"

Yeah, a part of her had. "I'll admit it's had some challenges." She felt a new wave of heat in her body that had nothing to do with the tequila and everything to do with Joe's touch. "I take it you ditched the Marshal keeping an eye on you. Otherwise, Harris and Walsh would probably already be beating down the door."

"The Marshals are good at stakeouts, but they suck at tailing people. Besides, the tracking device they put on my car was easy to spot and it's now on a garbage truck. By the way, I found the second one you left me as well. You didn't think you'd get away with that, did you?"

"A girl can hope, can't she?"

He took hold of her other wrist, rubbing the delicate skin inside with his thumb. "You're safe here, I swear. This place is completely off the books. Not even my brothers know about it."

The mystery deepened. A part of her wanted to crawl into his lap and lay her head on his shoulder. "I suppose you're going to be a complete gentleman and give me the bed?"

"I'm not much of a gentleman, but I'll take the couch."

She wanted to shake her head. She wanted to shake *him*. "First thing in the morning, I want to dig into both Dupé and Walsh." At his surprised expression, she continued, "Whoever set all this in motion has to be high up in the chain of command. There are several players between me and them, and I'll look into them, too, but whoever is the mastermind covered their tracks like an expert. There are plenty of talented people in the West Coast FBI, but not many could pull off anything of this caliber. It has to be someone who appears above reproach. Untouchable. That means they're at the top."

The idea that the director of the West Coast FBI or his counterpart at Homeland could be dirty screwed up his face. "We'll start first thing tomorrow."

Standing this close to him, his fingers wrapped around her wrist and her pulse beating far too fast, she longed to reverse the clock. Longed to go back to a place before she'd known she wasn't good enough for him.

For all her education and training, she never would be, regardless of her many accomplishments, commendations, or achievements. Joe was truly a hero, and she could never be worthy of him.

When she didn't move, he tugged her closer. She knew it was wrong, but her body defied her brain and she leaned down and kissed him.

Before she knew it, his arms were around her and he was pulling her into his lap, his hands no longer afraid of touching her. She reveled in the feel of him as he ravished her lips, nipping at her bottom one and trailing kisses across her jaw. He licked her earlobe and kissed down her neck, sweeping her hair out of the way. Her hips ground into his pelvis, and his hands went to them, urging her on.

As she began to unbutton his shirt, he took advantage of the invitation and lowered his head to her cleavage. Seven months without him had been too long. Despite her current situation, she was so hungry for his touch, for those lips. For his sheer and utter confidence.

Her shirt and bra came off with ease and landed on the floor. His shirt followed. Once his chest was bare, she pressed against him, wrapping her arms around his neck and burying her face in the crook of his neck. Her breasts pressed to his chest, and she could feel his heartbeat. He stopped moving, just holding her, as if tuning in to the shared moment.

The fire between her legs wouldn't let her rest. She was about to start shifting again, that bulge in his pants teasing her and making her ache, when his phone rang.

Panting, she jerked back, startled at the noise blasting through the semi-quiet kitchen. They both looked at it, and alarm bells rang in her head, seeing the ID.

Cooper Harris.

As if someone hit her with a cattle prod, she jumped off Joe's lap, scrambling to gather her clothes. "Why is he calling at this time of night?"

It was actually morning. One to be exact. Joe touched the edge of the cell, but didn't make a move to pick it up. "No idea."

Sam hated the fear in her voice, but she couldn't help it. "This can't be good."

Joe looked at her with steady eyes and motioned with his

free hand for her to relax. "You don't know that. Let me answer it, okay?"

Jack-Jack, who'd heard the noise, or maybe simply sensed her agitation, came padding into the kitchen. She slipped on her bra and threw the shirt on over it, before kneeling to pet him.

"Yeah, this is Cahill," Joe answered. "What's up, Agent Harris?"

Joe put the phone on speaker and Harris's voice, softer than Sam expected, said, "Sorry to disturb you. Hope you weren't sleeping."

"Nope. Just out driving the streets."

Sam thought Harris sounded as if he was trying not to wake somebody, his deep voice suppressed. "You couldn't sleep either?"

"I do some of my best work at night." Joe winked at her, and she tried not to roll her eyes at his double entendre. "Contrary to popular media, felons on the run rarely walk down the street in the bright light of day."

"So true," Harris said. "Say, do you know anything about a bunch of bombings up and down the coast Rosenthal was investigating before all this went down?"

Joe frowned and she felt a twinge in her gut. What was Harris looking into that for?

"Afraid not. Why? What's that got to do with apprehending our suspect?"

"Just a hunch I'm working on. The bombings don't seem to have a lot in common—different locations and perpetrators with no obvious connection, different kinds of bombs. They were all soft targets, but that's the only similarity. I'm wondering why Rosenthal brought this to the attention of her boss, Frank, and some of the other folks on the counterterrorism team."

Sam glanced around hurriedly. She needed a piece of paper

and a pen. There was none in obvious sight, but she'd seen a notebook in the office and ran to get it. From the kitchen, she heard Joe say, "Can you send me the list? I can look into it."

"I was thinking maybe you could come by tomorrow. Dinner at my house. I have a full day with some of our other cases, but I'd like to talk to you. Get a feel for your ex a little more."

Sam hustled back in, writing on the notebook. She had no idea how Harris had discovered this piece of trivia, and maybe it didn't matter, but she needed Joe to ask the right questions. She held up the notebook for him to read.

"These bombs." He squinted at her hasty penmanship. "You said they were soft targets?"

"Over the course of nine months, they all hit specific places where people were outside. There was a VA hospital opening a new wing, where a bomb was left in a car in the parking lot. It killed three and injured a dozen more gathered outside for the event. Another took place at a Memorial Day celebration. A third one at a mall, at a fundraiser held in the courtyard." The sound of shuffling papers. "There's more, and each of them different."

Joe stared at her as if he didn't get the connection either. She wrote one word on a clean sheet of paper and held it up. He frowned, and shook his head, still not understanding.

And then, as if the lightbulb went on, his face changed. "Veterans," he said. "Military personnel. Law enforcement. First responders, like the Aztec bombing. They were all *patriots*."

Harris was quiet for a tense moment, the silence weighted as he processed that information. "Gatherings like these always have law enforcement and security around. Lots of terrorists try to hit those types of targets."

Sam tapped the word on her notebook. Joe nodded. "And every one also featured active military or veterans, I bet. Again,

I know you're thinking that's not unusual for terrorists to pick on, but perhaps in this case, there's a deeper link."

"And that is?"

Her theory was too long to write out and she made a slashing motion across her neck. Joe understood, and played dumb. "Let me think about it and get back to you tomorrow. Dinner you said? Shoot me your address and the time. I'll be there."

Harris agreed and the two disconnected. Joe put down his phone. "Explain this connection to patriotism and the bombers," he said, pointing to her chair.

All she really wanted to do was crawl into bed with him, get some sleep, feel his arms around her. Instead, Sam launched into her next conspiracy theory.

13

Sam woke with bright light streaming into the room. The smell of coffee teased her nose and she found Joe placing a cup on the bedside table.

"Sorry," he said. "But it's time to get up, sleeping beauty."

Jack-Jack jumped on the bed and landed on her chest, making her *oomph*. She tried to move him aside. Undaunted, he began fervently licking her face, and she again, shoved at him, laughing. "Stop that," she chastised, even though she actually liked it.

She'd always wanted a dog, but her parents moved so much, they would never let her. Plus, because of their jobs, they were often gone and had to drop her at one of her grandparents' homes, or with people they trusted if they were out of town at the same time.

She rubbed sleep from her eyes. "What time is it?"

"Almost noon." Joe put his hands on his hips. "We need to go over a few things before I leave."

She reached for the coffee, and tried to keep her eyes off his chest. He was wearing nothing but jeans, his bare feet poking out from the bottom hems. She knew him well enough to know he was flaunting those hard pecs and chiseled abs intentionally. "Where are you going?"

Jack-Jack licked her ear, making her spill coffee. Joe chuckled. "I have to act normal, go about my day. It's not unusual for me to not go home at night, or be gone for a day or so when I'm chasing a bounty. But with all the scrutiny on me, I don't want to raise suspicions more than I already have."

She downed more of the warm coffee, enjoying the scent and taste. Such a simple thing, and yet, one she had missed to the extreme while on the run. "Are you seriously going to dinner at Harris's tonight?"

Joe strolled to the door, his gaze falling on the t-shirt and shorts she'd worn to bed. "Since I'm contracting for the task-force, I don't see that I have a lot of choice. I'm not sure what he's up to, but I doubt this is a friendly gathering. Harris and his team are smart. They want to pick my brain and see how loyal I am to the cause, I'm betting."

She rolled her shoulders, easing some of the stiffness. She hadn't slept that good in ages. "Let me take a shower and I'll be down."

"Another shower?"

She kissed Jack-Jack on the top of the head and stood, setting down the coffee to stretch. Sleeping in a bed, enjoying morning coffee, hot showers...she might never get enough of those small necessities of life again. "Yes. After you've been living on the streets this long without running water, you can criticize. Until then, shut up."

He chuckled and pointed at his bag that he'd thrown on the room's straight back chair in the corner. "Figured you might want to repack that and hide it outside somewhere for easy access. Under the back porch might be a good spot."

Giving her one last look at his broad chest, he grinned and left.

Jack-Jack stayed as she grabbed the cup and go-bag and proceeded to do exactly that.

Most of the original contents were still inside. She added items from the stashes of girly stuff in the bathroom, some yoga pants, a couple tank tops, and tampons. The bag held two Trac-Fones with phone cards, two waterproof bags surfers used to keep phones and valuables dry and free of sand, and his stun gun. There were also envelopes of cash in various denominations. Once she was satisfied, she placed it by the bedroom door and hopped in the shower.

After a too-brief rinse, she found Joe making pancakes, Jack-Jack at his feet in the kitchen. There was a plate of crispy bacon on the counter, and she was pretty sure the dog had already had a slice or two, but he was a bottomless pit.

She didn't blame him. Her stomach growled at the smell of the food and she made her way to the coffee pot to refill her empty cup.

Joe was still shirtless, the bastard. He gave her the side-eye, looking over her attire, and she tried to keep the grin off her face. Two could play at the silly seduction game. She'd found a pair of cutoff shorts, a tube top, and an oversized Roxy tank.

She'd scraped her wet hair into a tight ponytail at the back of her head after using temporary hair color to turn it a rich red.

In one of the costume drawers, she'd found colored contacts that turned her eyes a bright emerald green. She flashed her false lashes at Joe and leaned a hip against the counter. "Did you sleep okay on the couch?"

He flipped one of the cakes and nodded. "I assume you found the bed to your liking?"

The only thing that would've made it better was having him beside her. "Any news on Kyle's death?"

"It's been reported." He layered several pancakes on a plate and handed it to her. "Nothing so far has been leaked about his involvement with the government or you."

She accepted the breakfast and nearly tripped over Jack-Jack as the dog stayed right under her feet, hoping she might share. Maneuvering around him, she made it to the table, where butter, syrup, and assorted jellies were laid out. "Yet," she emphasized. "They may not plant that idea in the media, but I bet they have within the law organizations looking for me."

After turning off the stove, he grabbed his own plate, carrying the bacon with it. He sat down and started to dig in, and she sighed heavily, trying to keep her eyes off his chest. "Guess I'll find out when I talk to Walsh and Harris today," he said.

Hunger gnawing at her, she dug in as well, nearly swooning at the delicious food.

Joe consumed about half of his portion before he stopped, wiped his fingers on a napkin, sucked down some coffee, and began to nibble on a slice of bacon. "So if someone purposely instigated the bombings in all these different places in California, trying to target law enforcement, military, and first responders, what was their motivation?"

She swallowed a mouthful and followed it with coffee. "Funding. A biggie at the top of my list. After 9/11, we poured money into counterterrorism, both domestic and abroad, but in recent years, a lot of that's been diverted. Homeland and the other alphabet agencies claim we haven't had any major terrorist attacks on U.S. soil since, because of the efforts everyone's been making, but along with that comes a decrease in America's focus on the subject. Most counterterrorism organizations have seen funding sources dry up or be diverted to other areas."

She chewed on a slice of bacon. "People have been moved around and shifted into other departments. Walsh's domestic team is a fraction of what Homeland had here five years ago.

He's running a huge section of the country with a handful of people culled from the various organizations. Dupé's taskforces have dwindled from north to south, under orders of the Justice Department and FBI headquarters."

"You're suggesting treason." She could see skepticism in his face. "Someone behind the scenes starts blowing up soft targets throughout the state in order to cry terrorism and increase funding for security measures?"

She didn't care if he was skeptical. "Follow the money, Joe. It's happened before. The public doesn't hear about such stuff, but you and I both know it's a possibility. Look at urban crime and the war on drugs. Taskforces and law enforcement want citizens to feel secure, and they manipulate the numbers to make it look like violent crime is down or drug related crimes are static. Then, when the higher-ups have no facts to substantiate that gangs, drug dealers, and the violent crime rates are rising, what's the first thing they do? They beg for money, and our government sucks at doling it out. Cities and counties become gridlocked, even D.C. shuts down at times. Why? Because legislators can't pass a simple budget to keep their offices open. By the time they look at something like domestic terrorism, they don't have a clue how to budget for it. The only time they get into the nitty gritty is when there's an outcry from the public."

"That comes when people don't feel safe, and the best way to inspire terror is to threaten their homes, families, and independence."

"Exactly."

He finished off his slice of bacon. "And that's what you were investigating? Who did you suspect—the Bureau? Homeland?"

"That's what I was *trying* to investigate. Along with my undercover assignment with Jimmy T, I was slowly putting pieces together. When I took my preliminary findings to Frank, he laughed at me. Literally laughed. Called me paranoid and always trying to stir the pot. He said, 'I love you, Sammy girl, but this is nuts even for you.'"

Frank Jesson had taken Alison's place after she was fired.

Joe leaned back, grabbed a folder from the counter and slapped it on the table. Sam wiped off her fingers and lifted the flap to peek inside. The top sheet looked like an organizational chart of the FBI. There were X's through some of the names. "What's this?"

"I looked for connections and possibilities, running on your theory. Not just about who set you up with Jimmy T, but about this idea that someone on the inside was coordinating the bombings. These are the people I crossed off."

Most of those listed had a red X through them, including her boss, Frank, and several of the other mid-level managers. "I could have told you Frank and these others"—she pointed to several names—"couldn't have fallen into the suspect category."

"Frank was easy. I knew he didn't join the West Coast FBI until last fall."

When she and Joe were still together. The unsaid words hung in the air. "Of course." They'd talked about it in passing after Alison had been fired and Sam refused to take her job. "Would have been difficult for him to coordinate bombings that occurred earlier in the year from his previous post in the South. Besides, he was completely opposite to Alison. Very supportive. I was his favorite—he told me that many times."

"What about some of the others?" Joe stood to refill his coffee, and tried not to let the remark about Sam's boss tweak jealousy in him. The guy was old enough to be her dad, for Christ's sake. He was glad she'd had a decent superior after Alison had been such a train wreck. "I ruled out a few because they wouldn't have the means to pull off something as intricate as this. It would take someone inside the counterterrorism group, don't you think?"

She eyed the chart. "Definitely. Our suspect had to have

access to potential terrorists and a means of contacting them." Several were circled as possibilities. Two were on her list as well. "He or she needed access to databases as well as the physical contacts and resources."

Joe had been with the Bureau for nearly eight years before resigning. He was right about the perpetrator probably being in the counterterrorism department. Someone like him, who worked kidnappings and missing persons, would have little access to potential perpetrators or the ways to coordinate the bombings. There were still four people circled. The most logical made her stomach flip—Victor Dupé.

He was a god in the West Coast FBI, and although she'd never met him, she looked up to him. He seemed bigger than life, infallible, garnering the admiration and respect of everyone who worked under him. Plus, since he'd swept Olivia off her feet, Sam hated the idea he could be dirt.

Dr. Walsh had a similar fan club.

In Southern California, Dupé's taskforce, run by Harris, was one of the most widely recognized. The other teams sprinkled throughout Los Angeles, Sacramento, and further north were equally filled with highly trained individuals from the FBI, NSA, Homeland, ICE, and DEA.

They worked in conjunction with Walsh's Domestic Terrorism Taskforce, also revered throughout the state, but it seemed Walsh and Harris had a special camaraderie.

Walsh spent as much time south of L.A. as he did in the City of Angels. Of course, Southern California was rife with violence attributed to the border, gangs, and the drug pipeline coming up from South America. To say the SCVC Taskforce had its hands full was an understatement, and Walsh lent his team to them frequently.

There was a time when Sam had dreamed of joining one of them. Everyone there was an expert. Regardless of what organization they hailed from, they worked to form two well-oiled machines. It was one of things she'd always wanted to be part of.

But Dupé had repeatedly turned down her request to the join the SCVC, ignoring her reports. Or maybe he never saw them, thanks to Alison. Even Frank said he didn't want to lose her. Maybe everything Sam turned in CC'd to the director got tossed in the garbage or shredded.

It would literally ruin her if she found out Dupé wasn't the hero everyone believed him to be, but she'd seen it happen. Heard her parents' stories about the traitors within the CIA, FBI, even the NSA. Yes, they were few and far between, but sometimes the more powerful they were, the more untouchable they believed themselves to be.

Joe brought the pot to the table and refilled her cup. He motioned at the pan that held a few remaining pancakes as if to ask if she wanted more.

She did, but she was stuffed, and now her brain was working on the possible traitor amongst them. Plus, she still needed to track down Kyle's girlfriend/assassin. She shook her head. After not eating much for the past few weeks, she'd consumed more than her shrunken stomach could handle.

"What are your plans for this afternoon?" she asked.

"Head back to my condo, check in with my brothers, do more digging on all of this." He waved his hand over the file. "We should have the tox screen on Kyle today, and I wanna be sure I touch base with Harris about the possibility he was murdered."

"I want to take some stuff to Hetty and Dec," she said sipping at the coffee. "You can drop me off at the bridge before you head to your apartment."

His gaze touched her hair, her eyes, her bare arms. "No dice. Remember our agreement? You're staying here, out of sight, regardless of the getup."

She met his gaze. "I can't just sit here on my ass and do nothing."

He shrugged, as if he couldn't care less what she thought. "That's the deal if you want to stay in my beautiful safe house with all the food you can eat."

His face was inscrutable, but she heard the underlying teasing there anyway. He loved when he had some control over her, which was almost never. "You need to put the go-bag under the back porch."

"Sure. Anything else?"

"How do you know I won't take off when you leave?"

"I know how big that brain of yours is, and that you'll accomplish more sitting at my computer today than running around San Diego looking for a ghost in the wind who might've murdered Kyle."

"You're going to let me use your computer?"

"I assume you're going to hack into some things I don't want to know about, so do me a favor and cover your tracks, okay?"

She grinned. "Least I can do after you fed me and let me shower."

He placed his plate into the sink, snagged the last piece of bacon, and took his cup as he left the kitchen. "The least you can do is the dishes."

As he headed toward the bedroom, Jack-Jack barked at her, as if agreeing. She rolled her eyes and called after Joe, "The least you can do is put a shirt on."

14

———

*N*orth San Diego

Joe parked in the condo's lot and locked up. Inside the main hallway Ted and Tony, his neighbors, passed him, the former carrying a paddleboard.

"Hey, bounty hunter," Tony quipped, looking him over. "You don't happen to find lost bikes, do you?"

Joe paused, flipping through his keyring for his house key. God, he hated the BH moniker, but he held his tongue. He tried not to let the rush he felt show on his face. "Lost bikes?"

Ted, a true SoCal looking blond, balanced the paddleboard on one knee and swept his long hair from his eyes. "Somebody stole mine the other night."

Tony—a dark, swarthy guy—gave his partner the stink eye. "If you'd locked it up like I told you to…"

Crap. Was the bike in the trunk of his car Tony's? "I'm afraid lost items are out of my realm of expertise, but I'll keep an eye out. Probably a kid used it to get to the beach. I'm sure it'll turn up."

Ted gave a thumbs-up, Tony waved, and the two thanked him before heading off.

Joe continued on to his door. The building's maintenance man was on a short stepladder, fiddling with an overhead light.

Except the body shape was wrong. The hair too.

Joe's internal warning system went off. "Where's Carlson?" he asked offhandedly as he stuck his key in the lock.

"Be back tomorrow," the man said, but his voice wasn't right.

Joe faced him. "Is that so?"

It was only then, when they locked eyes, he realized it wasn't a man.

The mustache was high quality, but a fake. The woman had darkened her eyebrows, and wore a wig. Her glasses were heavy framed.

He almost went for his gun, but then she smiled and muttered, "Did the camel drink the water?"

He glanced down the hallway, making sure Ted and Tony were out of sight. The partners had disappeared and he faced the fake maintenance man who happened to be Samantha's mother. "I almost shot you. I thought you might be an assassin."

A grin, and she fiddled with the overhead light. "I am, or was, but you're safe, kiddo. I promise."

He chuckled. "Our camel did, indeed, drink the water."

She paused a moment and nodded. "I'm so relieved. Now we just have to keep her at the well."

"Doing my best."

Val used a screwdriver to reattach the cover, and climbed down. "Does she know about the house? Where you got it?"

He could see the relief now, and also the worry. "She's curious, but I avoided getting into it." They'd had a lot of other things to talk about. "When the time is right, I'll fess up."

Val busied herself with her toolbox. "She'll guess before you tell her."

"Give me some credit here. I can handle her."

A rewarding smile. "Thank you. I owe you big for watching out for my girl. She's means everything to me."

"Me too."

"One day, I hope you'll forgive each other." She nodded. "I'll be in touch."

He watched her leave before letting himself inside. Sam's mother was as unique as she was. The house was the least of it. Val had known her daughter would never reach out to her when everything went down, would never put her in danger or make herself an easy target. Val knew better than to contact him directly, as well. Somebody somewhere was always watching. Listening. That was her take on life.

But she was as cunning and street-smart as Sam—no wonder Sam was so good undercover. Long before all this had happened, she'd given Joe a set of directions and they'd made backup plans in case anything happened to her, him, or Samantha.

Thank goodness they had. While they'd never anticipated this scenario, the old spy's strategy had come in handy.

He tossed his keys on the breakfast bar, unloaded his weapon, and saw the light blinking on his answering machine.

The message was from his brother, and when Joe heard it, he checked his cell. Sure enough, Caleb had called three times last night, and unable to raise him on that, tried his landline. Joe was going to the Bondsman Brothers office next, but first he had a little digging to do on Alison.

The place seemed too quiet, too empty, without Sam and Jack-Jack. Funny how he'd never gotten used to her absence to begin with, but after having her back, even for such a brief time, it was if the place sighed with the same relief he'd felt. Now, it felt forlorn all over again.

In the bedroom, he opened his nightstand drawer and withdrew a photo of them from a secret compartment Sam had purposely built into it. Normally, he kept the picture out, but after the bombing and her name becoming mud, he'd made sure to put any personal items of hers away. His only hope at helping her had been to appear completely neutral, if not antagonistic, toward her.

Yes, he was bait, but he had to make it as realistic as possible. They would have never let him go after her if they knew he still had feelings for her.

And he suspected somebody had been through his condo. No doubt they were checking all his calls and keeping tabs on the landlines at the office as well, on the off-chance Sam reached out to anybody who could get a message to him.

She hadn't said a word about their make-out session last night, and he was damned disappointed. He'd hoped they might do it again this morning. It had been a long dry spell since she'd left, and he was still helplessly in love with her.

He'd pulled out all the stops, flashing as much skin as he could, making her favorite breakfast, giving her the password to his computer. He'd even allowed her continued access to his go-bag, and did as she asked, placing it covertly under the back porch.

Knowing Sam, she probably had several places where she'd buried treasure. Not because she was a criminal, but she'd grown up with parents who'd taught her every spy trick in the book, and created a world where Sam always had multiple contingencies for any situation—no matter how extreme—to get away, stay under the radar, or do what needed to be done.

If the go-bag was in the bedroom and someone came through the front door while she was in the kitchen or bath, she'd have to leave it. If she put it by the back door and someone came in that way, ditto. She'd taught him long ago it was always good to have emergency supplies stashed outside the home, just in case.

It wasn't just about someone coming after you, but even in the case of fire, or a natural disaster. Having a minimum of supplies off-site sounded like an extreme survivalist way of living, but for Sam, it was normal. It's what helped her to sleep at night.

"God, you're so fucked up," he said to her picture. "And I mean that in the best way possible."

On the drive back to San Diego, he'd mentally reviewed various scenarios about Kyle, Jimmy T, and the slim thread that connected a series of six bombs in the past year. None of Sam's theories were that far out of the ballpark. The FBI was well known for former Director Robert Hanssen, who'd been selling secrets to Russia for years before someone finally blew the whistle on him.

There were plenty of conspiracy theories circling the world, and others that never saw the light of the day, that were based in absolute truth. He'd seen and heard more in the FBI than he cared to think about.

While he was able to compartmentalize most, continuing to believe in the moral and ethical people who populated the Bureau and Homeland, that five or ten percent who were borderline criminals themselves, if not outright threats to the country, occupied Sam's mind night and day. She was all about taking down terrorists, from within or without.

Returning the photo to his hiding spot inside the drawer, he grabbed a handful of jerky strips from his pantry and an energy drink. If he was going to be bait for everybody, he might as well do a little himself.

On his computer, he called up a search engine and went looking for Alison. Thanks to the wonders of the internet, he found her within thirty seconds.

"There you are," he said, clicking on the link to Lifeline Investigations.

Alison was a lead investigator for a PI firm these days, her bright shiny face looking back at him from the company's employee page. It was a decent size organization, with a variety of investigators handling everything from messy divorces to employee theft and other more serious crimes.

She looked older than he remembered, but the photographer had done a good job touching up wrinkles and coaxing a smile from her. Joe was pretty sure he never saw her smile the whole time he was in the FBI.

It took him a minute to mentally write the script of what he was going to say in his head, and another to get his mind in the right place to pull this off. He had to be as convincing as possible, and the idea of playing on her cougar advances to him made him ill. But he needed to rule her out for sure. Needed to ease his mind that she wasn't behind all of this.

She'd been a formidable person inside the San Diego branch of the FBI. She'd hailed from Los Angeles and was supposed to fix a handful of issues when she arrived in town. Her immediate boss was still in Los Angeles and reported to Dupé, and from what Joe had surmised during his time, she planned to rise up the ranks all the way to the top.

Before he called, he texted Caleb to tell him everything was cool. His brother was still unhappy and let him know it, but Joe promised to stop by as soon as he was done with his call.

A receptionist answered and he had to wait an additional minute and a half before Alison came on the line. "Joseph Cahill," her voice purred. "To what do I owe the pleasure?"

Joe forced himself to smile in order to convey happiness through the line. "How are you, Alison? Looks like you're doing well for yourself."

"My skills and talents are underserved here, but I'm working on something bigger. For now, this will do. Are you looking for a private investigator?"

"You know what happened with Sam, right?"

There was a pregnant pause, as if Alison were choosing her words carefully. "Doesn't everyone?" A hard edge entered her tone. "Surely, you don't expect me to help you find *her*? Although that would be a coup for me, wouldn't it?"

"I don't believe anyone's gonna find her. Actually, I was hoping we could get together over drinks. There's a lot of water under the bridge, but I'd like to clean some of it up. There are occasions when my brothers and I need a private investigator. I can't think of anyone more qualified."

"You want to have drinks to talk about collaborating?" She chuckled. "I know you better than that, Joe. What's this really about?"

This was where he had to make sure he came across believable.

Reluctantly, he took himself back to New Year's Day. Remembered the argument with Sam, the way she'd left. Everything in him wanted to freeze up, block it out, but he forced himself to breathe and let it in. "Look, Sam suckered all of us, especially me. I was hoping we could get past what happened when I was at the Bureau. I won't lie, I have a thing for smart, strong women, and I realize now I may have let one of the best get by me."

He was talking about Sam, but Alison didn't realize it. "If you're looking for absolution, you came to the wrong person. That bitch got me fired, ruined my career."

"We have that in common. I quit because I thought she was my perfect mate. Turns out, she was using me. I don't need absolution, but I would like to see you."

Another pause, one that held a scale. Alison was weighing his arguments against her own deep-seated distrust of him. He needed to play this carefully.

"You're right. This is a bad idea," he said, trying to sound regretful even as he imagined strangling her. "You don't owe me anything, but I do want to apologize for any role I played in Sam's quest to take you down."

That perked her interest. "That little bitch wanted my job

from the beginning. Thought she could do things better than I could." He heard her shift the phone, the sound of her chair squeaking softly as she rocked in it. "Tell you what, I will meet you for drinks. If nothing else, we could both use it to vent over her."

He slowly released a mental breath. "I have a dinner engagement tonight, but I'm free afterwards? You game?"

"Absolutely." She was back to purring, offering her cell number. "Text me the details and I'll be there."

The line went dead and he slid the phone onto his desktop leaned back, trying to relax his tense muscles.

He purposefully shook off the revolting feeling in his stomach. This was why Sam did the undercover work. He was better at straightforward interaction, not this covert game of pretending to be someone he wasn't.

The rest of the afternoon he spent checking in with his brothers, reading the analysis on Kyle that Harris emailed him, and updating both him and Walsh about some bogus tracking he'd supposedly been doing on Sam.

The tox screen was the most interesting thing of all of it. While Homeland and the FBI had no intention of releasing the information to the public, Sam was right.

Kyle Dunmire did *not* have an allergic reaction or food poisoning from the sushi.

He'd been deliberately poisoned.

15

───────

arlsbad

"Take off your shirt."

Joe was picking out a pair of dress pants to wear and flashed her a lazy grin. "You wanted me to put it on this morning, and now you want me to take it off?"

It was nearly seven and he was due at the Harris residence for dinner. Sam had spent all afternoon on his computer, following minuscule leads, and trying to identify who poisoned Kyle. "I'm putting a wire on you, whether you like it or not."

Jack-Jack lay sprawled on his side on the bed, watching and listening, his one visible eye moving back and forth as they argued.

Joe shook his head. "No dice. I don't need it, you're not listening, and besides, knowing Harris, he probably has some kind of radar detection and would discover it."

Sam fiddled with the tiny microphone and receiver. "I need peace of mind. You're also wearing an earbud, so if I hear anything that sparks a question, I can feed it to you."

He withdrew a pair of gray slacks. "I'm not going bugged. I'm trying to get him, Walsh, and Dupé to trust me. If they find out I walked into this dinner meeting"—he emphasized dinner —"with a wire and earbud, what little trust they may have goes up in smoke. Because why else would I have it unless you weren't listening in?"

She held up a hand. "No one has your back, except me." She'd stewed about this all afternoon, and this was the best way she could find to insert herself into it and make sure she covered him. "We already believe Harris is suspicious, and his taskforce is using you to get to me. Tonight will either confirm or refute that. There's no way he'll know you're wearing a wire. It's supposed to be a friendly dinner, and I'm guessing, all he wants is to figure out your emotional status when it comes to me."

Joe ran a hand over his face. Since he'd rushed in a few minutes ago, she'd suspected he was keeping something from her. The only thing he'd shared with her throughout the afternoon was the fact the tox screen confirmed the poison in Kyle's body. "Exactly. My emotional state is fine, and I know how to bluff about you."

Without waiting for her argument, he turned on his heel and stomped into the bathroom. Sam grabbed the wire and medical tape, then followed.

She startled him when she threw open the door, walked in, and hefted herself onto the vanity countertop. "I'm not letting you leave unless you wear it."

She said it smugly, as if she could actually prevent him from going out the front door.

Calling her bluff, he dropped his jeans and went to work putting the slacks on. "I'm not scared of you, Sam. As I recall, you've tried to keep me from doing things before. How did that work out?"

Was he keeping score? "Okay, sure. There may have been a time or two, but you did worse. You kidnapped me."

He threw his hands in the air. "That was one time. I was

trying to get you to relax. I hardly believe kidnapping you in order to take you on a weekend getaway qualifies as forcing you to do anything you didn't want to do."

He sort of had her there. Their weekend vacation in the hills of Northern California had been a treat, even though at first, she wanted to kill him for tricking her into believing they were just going out for dinner.

She'd spent the entire weekend without her laptop or the charger for her phone. He'd insisted on forty-eight hours with no connection to the outside world, and after she'd finally admitted she was at his mercy, it had been an awesome weekend.

He went to the double closets between the bedroom and bath. He slid through several hangers and pulled off a button-down shirt. He came back into the bathroom, tossed the fresh shirt at her, and peeled off the polo he was wearing.

She sighed, his beautiful chest and flat stomach trying to sidetrack her like always. The rest of him was as well, thighs muscled from daily runs, a tight ass, slim waist...

Focus. "Look, I know you plan to charm your way through this dinner, but Harris will be looking for any chink in your armor. Won't it help if you know I'm listening and can guide you with questions or comments that you might need help with?"

He looked at her as if he didn't understand what her problem was. He balled up the shirt and threw it in the laundry basket. "I'm stupid, but pretty, is that it? Plus, I have a great personality, right?"

He wasn't really angry, she could tell by the sarcastic tone. "You're extremely smart, the charm and beauty add to the total package."

She was going to say something else but he stalked across the floor and came to stand right in front of her. He needed the dress shirt she held, but he didn't reach for it.

Instead, he leaned forward, putting his face in front of hers, his big hands on either side of her thighs. "A total package you walked away from."

She was sorry about that, and if the situation were different, she'd reconsider her stupidity. She didn't have many regrets in life, but leaving him was one of them.

Now, however, she was a wanted fugitive on the run. She had no one and nothing. Not even her brains, or her training, could guarantee she'd get out of this one.

Reaching up, she touched his cheek. "I was an idiot. Pretty, but stupid."

She gave him a sad grin.

He leaned in and kissed her, and she let him. She realized this afternoon the safe house, the food, even the hot showers were perks, but the real reason she stayed was because of Joe.

The kiss went from hot to scalding instantly and Sam dropped the shirt. Joe grabbed her hips, scooting her toward him. Their bodies slammed together, pelvis to pelvis, and she sucked in a breath.

She ran her hands over his naked chest, down his arms, up to his strong neck. His tongue plunged in her mouth and he pushed her back so far, her head was nearly touching the mirror behind them.

She couldn't get enough of him, running her fingers in his short hair and groaning as she pressed her breasts against his chest.

Strong fingers held her in place, his obvious erection teasing her through his slacks and her yoga pants. The thinnest of materials, but the hottest of needs. Wrapping her legs around him, she moaned as they fit together perfectly and that heat made her nearly orgasm on the spot.

His hands rose, fingers brushing her ribs until they found her breasts. As he kissed her chin, and trailed his way along her jawline, he teased her nipples, drawing small mewing sounds from her. She forgot who she was, where she was, what she was running from. Time and space meant nothing—she was Joe's.

A beeping noise echoed through the room, jerking Sam out of the Joe-induced fog. He tensed, and murmured close to her ear. "Aw, shit."

The alarm he'd set to keep him on time. He drew back, glanced at his watch. "I'm late." He kissed her on the end of the nose. "We will resume this later."

He reached for the shirt on the floor, now wrinkled. Jack-Jack appeared in the door and gave a bark, as if telling him to get a move on.

Sam swore under her breath. She'd been this close to an orgasm and he hadn't even gotten her out of her clothes. She tore the shirt from his hands and held it away from him. "Unh unh. You're not going anywhere without the wire."

He started to argue, and Jack-Jack barked again, this time louder. He probably thought this was an invitation to play, but it distracted them for a second. When Joe's gaze flicked back to her, he sighed loudly. "Fine, but make it quick."

She did. As she finished taping the mic to his chest, he said, "After the dinner, I have another meeting."

Tossing the wrinkled dress shirt in the laundry basket, she grabbed a turquoise blue button-down from the closet and handed it to him. "With who?"

He set his jaw, gritting his teeth hard enough to make a tiny muscle under his cheekbone dance. "No one important. But I will be taking this mic off and earbud out, so don't freak."

Warning bells rang in her head. "Oh, I see." The bells triggered her stomach to flip flop as well. "This person wouldn't happen to be the mistress you kicked out of here, would it?" She teased. Acting jealous might be the only way to find out the truth.

"Oh, hell no. Let's just say I have an idea and I want to follow it through."

He was being too secretive, and it didn't sit well with her. She'd already forced him to wear the wire, how much more could she push?

Returning to her side of the closet, she switched out her clothes for dark leather pants and a black t-shirt. "I don't care who it is, I'm coming with you. I'll stay in the car while you're at Harris's, then I'll watch your back during whatever this other meeting is."

He yanked on dress shoes and shook his head. "You are *not* coming with me."

"Yes, I am." She pulled the t-shirt over her head and shoved her feet in soft leather joggers "Ninja Sam is ready."

He walked by, the corner of his mouth quirking as he eyed her attire. "Ninja or not, you're staying here."

Jack-Jack looked between them, stretching out on his front paws, tail in the air wagging. He thought they were still playing, and he was happy to join in. As Joe went to the bedroom door, Jack-Jack ran after him.

So did Sam. Following Joe and the dog through the house, she smiled to herself. "You can't make me stay here. Besides, it's time for the Joe Cahill - Samantha Rosenthal team to resurrect their partnership."

At the front door, he snatched his keys and wallet from the hall table and stuck them in his pockets. "Sam..."

She grabbed his arm, made him look at her. "I am going with you."

Sam couldn't control him, couldn't really control the situation, and she hated it. It was one thing to get herself into a pickle, but now Joe was in it with her, and she intended to do everything in her power to protect him. When the shit finally hit the fan, whatever the outcome, she needed to make sure the collateral damage to him was as little as possible.

"There's one thing," she said. "No matter what happens, will you get a message to my mom?"

It was subtle, but his face changed. A slight tension in his body shifted. For a second, she almost felt like he was throwing shutters over a window, trying to keep her from seeing a truth. "Of course."

"If something should happen to me—"

His face hardened. "Nothing is going to. I promise."

His bravado was appreciated, but they both knew this was a no-win situation. Proving her innocence was growing harder than the already impossible task it'd been to begin with.

"Every law enforcement officer in the country is looking for me, and ninety percent of them would love to put a bullet in me. Things happen, and if the person behind all of this wants to silence me, they're going to make sure I never go to prison. That I never get to tell the truth about what I did and didn't do."

He opened his mouth to argue but she cut him off. "Just tell Mom I'm sorry for screwing up. Tell her...how much I love her, and I'm sorry for leaving her like dad."

Her dad had died unexpectedly, and not from any crazy situation like this, but simply because of a stupid drunk driver. All his life, all the dangerous missions he'd been on, to end up dying like that made her sick.

Her mother had been devastated, never the same afterwards. The only people in the world she still trusted were Sam and her brothers. Mother and daughter had always been so close, and now Valerie Rosenthal didn't have Sam either. Might never see her again.

Joe faced her, grabbing both her arms with his strong hands and giving her a hard shake. "You're going to tell her that yourself, and you're not leaving her. You're going to be together again, I swear it."

She couldn't help herself, couldn't deny how much she loved this man in front of her. She wrapped her arms around his neck and kissed him, making him even later.

"We can't do this," Sam said breathlessly, and Joe kissed her to shut her up.

He planned to keep right on doing it so she couldn't change her mind. Hell, he'd strip and do a Magic Mike impression—mesmerize her with his chest, abs, whatever—if he could keep her from second-guessing what they were about to do.

He backed her against the foyer wall, rattling the mirror hanging there. Jack-Jack whimpered and Joe chased him off by throwing a nylon bone from the foyer table into the living room.

As the dog happily scampered after it, Joe lifted Sam. Her legs went around his hips and he groaned at their fit, pressing his already hard erection into her.

She broke from his kiss. "You're going to wrinkle that shirt." But her argument was weak since she was running her hands down his back and squeezing his ass.

"There are a dozen more in the closet," he told her.

"So we can tear each other's clothes off at least eleven more times and you'll still have a decent shirt to wear to dinner."

He laughed, rocking his hard-on into her. "How about we

just do this right here, right now." He nuzzled her ear and loved how she arched into him. "Then again, later, a dozen times."

She gripped the lapels of the shirt and gave a yank, sending the buttons flying. Her eyes feasted on his chest, even with the mic taped to it. "I'm game if you are."

Her lips found his collarbone and he braced his hands on the wall behind her, keeping her pinned to it with his hips. He wanted inside her now, but they had so much time to make up for. He needed to make this last, give her everything she loved and more.

Soft fingers trailed over his pecs, down his abdomen. She kissed his neck, ran her tongue over the muscles there. Her teeth nibbled his earlobe.

He nearly exploded right there.

"I'm sorry for leaving," she whispered in his ear. "It was a huge mistake."

"Damn right it was." He tugged the ponytail out and let the strands skim over his hands. He loved her hair. "But what's done is done. I was wrong to insist you stop undercover work, but I was scared, Sam. Scared you'd get killed."

Her hand stroked the side of his face. "I know."

No more words were needed. They worked frantically at removing their clothes, Joe putting her down long enough to peel the yoga pants off her, kissing her thighs as he went. She ran her hands through his short hair and soon he had her against the wall again, his mouth finding the soft folds between her legs.

The smell of her filled his nose, his tongue focusing on that sensitive nub of hers. She cried his name, arching and rocking, matching the tempo he built. Slipping two fingers inside her, he relished her reaction, feeling her muscles grip him, the onslaught of her orgasm a speeding train rushing for the peak of the mountain. When it hit, she jerked hard, and he rode it with her, teasing it out.

Her legs went weak, and he eased her to the floor, mouthing each breast in turn, licking all her sensitive spots. She shivered under his ministrations, then she begged for more.

He obliged, bringing her to climax several more times with his fingers and mouth, until she claimed she couldn't stand any more.

She lied.

Next thing he knew, he was on his back, the tile of the floor cool under his shoulder blades and butt. Sam straddled his straining erection, hovering over it for a long heartbeat and licking her lips before meeting his eyes and beginning to lower herself.

Inch by teasing inch, she dragged it out, eyes half-lidded as they searched his. Her lips parted in an O, her sensitive skin engorged, squeezing his cock tight.

He thought he'd burst from the slick, white heat of her as she worked his shaft with practiced skill. Hands on her breasts, he watched her face, loving how expressive she was with every stroke. Her long hair hung down, teasing his face.

She braced her hands on his chest and began a slow, tantalizing dance, bringing him to the point of no return over and over. Each time he was at his edge, she'd back off just enough to string him along.

He was a patient man, and he wanted to give her whatever she wanted, but he finally reached the breaking point.

Gripping her hips with his legs, and protecting her upper body with his muscled arms, he twisted, putting her under him once again. He couldn't hold back, and she didn't want him to.

She met every stroke as he ground into her, nails digging into his shoulders, head thrown back in ecstasy. Her hips rocked with his tempo, soft words of encouragement speeding both of them headlong into the abyss.

He loved every inch of her beautiful body. Knew it better

than he did his own. When he sensed her release coming, he kept his gaze locked on hers and lowered his mouth to kiss her.

I love you, Sam, he tried to convey. *I'm never letting you go again.*

The orgasm hit and she clamped her legs tight around his waist, crying his name once more, the force of it echoing through the house.

Teasing it out for her, he found he couldn't hold back any longer. He let himself plunge over the sweet edge of bliss with her.

Joe arrived late but hell if it wasn't worth it.

Thomas Mann greeted him at the door, ushering him in and taking the bottle of wine he'd picked up. Luckily, Cooper's place was only a few miles from the safe house and there was a convenience store on the way. Sam had insisted he not show up emptyhanded.

Yes, he'd caved and let her come. He feared if he didn't, she'd find a way to follow him anyway. Right now, she was outside, probably casing the place and ignoring his orders to stay hidden in the car.

Ronni brushed by him with several bowls of steaming rice and vegetables to set on a long, dining table. "Cahill," she said with a nod.

He was introduced to Nelson Cruz and Sophie Diaz. Cruz was part of the taskforce, Diaz was his wife and an FBI agent. Each held one of their twins and a bottle, so they all skipped shaking hands, since theirs were full.

Mann led him to the kitchen. Cooper was on the patio grilling steak, Celina informed him, as she drew a beer from the fridge and handed it to him. Ronni made the formal introductions, but Celina gave Joe a hug as if they were old friends, before she began stirring what smelled liked seasoned chicken on the stove.

A young boy chased a toddler past Joe's legs, a tiny chihuahua barking at them as they raced through.

"That's Owen and Princess Via," Thomas said. "They belong to Coop and Celina."

"And Thunder," Ronni shoved a bowl of shredded lettuce at him. "The dog. Put that on the table, would you?"

Beer in one hand, the lettuce in the other, Joe followed Mann to the dining room. An older guy in a wheelchair sat at one end, a woman who introduced herself as Eliza, and the man, her husband, as Bobby Dyer.

"Your ex is in a boat-load of shit," Bobby said, and Joe laughed, immediately liking him.

"She is that."

Further discussion of Sam was forestalled when one of the twins spit up on Nelson and he hurriedly carried the baby—holding it at arm's length—to the bathroom, while Via screamed at the top of her lungs over something Owen did and the dog went crazy barking. Although Joe did hear Sam list all the exits, just in case, and describe the layout of the house as if she were inside.

With everyone distracted, he moved to look out a window and murmured, "You're not in here, right? I told you to stay in the car."

Her reply was a soft laugh.

The disarray and mayhem, along with the delicious smells of the food, triggered memories of his mom's regular Sunday night dinners that he and his brothers were obligated to attend and never minded at all.

Cooper walked in carrying a tray with still sizzling sliced steak. "Glad you made it, Cahill. Have a seat."

Celina appeared with the chicken, and the others helped

carry in the rest, including soft tortilla shells, salsa, guacamole, and other condiments. "I decided to keep it easy," Celina said, "so we're doing a taco bar."

Nelson returned and the twins were placed in their car seats, Via in a high chair, and the others gathered around the table.

Dishes were passed, and Joe loaded his plate. In his ear, he heard Sam complain. "I can smell the grilled meat. I'm jealous. Eat a taco for me, too."

Whatever else happened tonight, he was definitely going to enjoy the food.

Stories about the kids and family life were shared, reminding Joe again of his own family. His mom had always been a big cook, and liked to feed her husband and three boys with similar meals.

During a pause in conversation, Celina handed Via several crackers and eyed him. "Joe, your accent isn't SoCal. Where are you from?"

He swallowed and wiped his lips with his napkin. "Grew up on the east coast, mostly around D.C. and Virginia."

"How'd you end up here?" Thomas queried.

"You know the Bureau. They sent me as far away from home as they could get, outside of Alaska or Hawaii."

All three of the FBI agents chuckled at the joke.

"Why did you leave it for bounty hunting?" Eliza asked.

He forced himself not to cringe at the term. She seemed genuinely interested, but Joe suspected someone had planted that question for her to raise.

He smiled and sipped his beer. "I was getting burned out, and my brothers needed help. The first skip trace I did for free, but I found I liked it. I wouldn't tell them that, of course, at least not for a while. But eventually, I took more and more cases, enjoying fugitive apprehension best, and when they offered me a full-time job, I accepted."

Ronni rose and went to the kitchen, bringing back the open bottle of wine and refilling her glass. She motioned, but no one else wanted any. "Seems a lot different than the Bureau."

"As an agent, I was in kidnapping. Searching for missing kids or tracking fugitives—it works the same for me. Guess I like the chase, and seem to have the skills to find people."

"Any luck hunting down Rosenthal?" Cruz asked. All eyes pinned Joe.

"I found someone who'd seen her living under a bridge south of town, but it seems she hasn't been there in days."

Ronni started to ask another question and Cooper cleared his throat. His gaze went to Owen and Via, and she shifted gears, taking the conversation back to something non-work related.

Joe heard a whining sound and looked down to find the chihuahua at his feet. The dog's big, brown eyes stared at him with an eagerness he'd seen in Jack-Jack. He was begging for food, and Joe tried to ignore him.

They finished eating, discussing the weather, the latest shark sighting at the beach, and the Padres' losing streak. Eventually, the meal wrapped up and Joe started helping Celina and Ronni clear plates.

The twins had fallen asleep and Sophia laid them on a rug in the living room after Nelson and Thomas moved the coffee table out of the way. Thunder crawled between the babies and nestled down. Via started crying and Celina paced the hall, soothing her. Cooper mentioned she was cutting teeth and all the other parents nodded in understanding.

Owen begged Cooper to go outside and toss a frisbee, the long days a boon to the boy. Thomas volunteered to do it and they took off, Thunder going with them.

The atmosphere was definitely family-oriented. Everyone seemed at home in Cooper and Celina's house, and as Ronni got a pot of decaf coffee going, Eliza and Sophia loaded the dishwasher, and Bobby cleaned the table.

A platter of cookies was brought out, along with some mugs. Nelson sat next to Bobby and they began discussing a case the taskforce was working on.

Cooper went out to clean the grill and cover it, and returned a few minutes later with Thomas and a laughing Owen.

The boy snatched a cookie from the plate before Cooper chased him off to get ready for bed. Once the kid said good-night to everyone, he disappeared to the back of the house. Celina, who'd apparently gotten Via asleep, came out and grabbed a cookie herself. "Fingers crossed she doesn't wake until dawn."

Thomas slouched in a chair and spoke to Joe. "Glad you could come. We didn't get to talk at the meeting the other day."

Joe resumed his original seat. "The life of an FBI agent," he said good-naturedly. "You never know when things are going to break or you need to pick up a warrant."

"True that." Ronni brought in a trivet and the decaf coffee. She helped herself to a cup and offered one to Bobby, who nodded.

"What about me?" Thomas asked her.

"Bobby broke that encrypted file for me today that I need-ed." She sat and grinned at him. "And you're capable of getting your own."

Cooper resumed his seat at the head of table. Joe had to laugh when Ronni poured him a cup and carefully slid it down to his end, while Thomas harrumphed.

They weren't just a taskforce, they were family.

Cooper kicked back in his chair and eyed Joe. "I'm actually surprised you came."

Joe hadn't expected Cooper's candor. "I am, too," he replied. "I assume this is more than a friendly get-together."

Bobby dug into a leather case hanging on his wheelchair,

producing two sets of documents. He pushed one across the table to Joe.

"The first rule of engagement," Cooper said, "is that everything discussed at the table goes no farther until I'm sure we have all our ducks in a row. Agreed?"

Everyone nodded, then looked at Joe. He wasn't sure what they were going to discuss, but he did the same as if he understood where the conversation was going. They were getting down to business, and apparently, he was in the spotlight.

"What's this?" he asked of the papers in front of him.

Bobby motioned at Thomas to give him a cookie. Thomas put one on a napkin and slid it over to him. "Rosenthal's former boss, Alison Kendrick, ran that analysis on Rosenthal before the Aztec bombing using Kyle Dunmire's software. That is an original, and it shows Rosenthal was less than two percent likely to commit a terrorist act. There doesn't seem to be any order from higher up the chain for that report to be run. Kendrick ordered it."

Joe shrugged. "When I spoke to Kyle, he mentioned that the software was often used to analyze agents, especially those in the field, as well as potential terrorists." He glanced around. "I wouldn't be surprised if they've run this on all of you. According to the kid, it was something they were looking into, like doing background checks. It's part of a preemptive strategy the FBI and Homeland have implemented, even though they can't use it to discriminate against you."

Glances were exchanged. Dyer tapped the second report still in front of him. "The interesting thing is that Kendrick put together a report after the Aztec bombing, and in it was the analysis about Rosenthal. This one, however, states Rosenthal was *fifty-two* percent likely to commit a terrorist act."

Bobby slid the report to Joe.

"That bitch," Sam said in his ear. "She is behind this, but how?"

Joe looked at the two reports, noting the highlighted areas showing the differences. "So you're suggesting it was tampered with?"

"Obviously," Ronni said. "But by whom? Kendrick is the clear winner if we only look at this piece of the puzzle, but she doesn't fit with some of the other things we know."

The wheels in Joe's head spun. "Excuse me for asking, but what does this have to do with me bringing Sam in?"

Cooper sat forward and played with his cookie. He still hadn't taken a bite yet. "Stay with us, here. I promise, we have a reason for the interrogation."

"We know about the background between you and Samantha," Thomas said. "We also know what happened with her and Kendrick."

Ronni sipped her coffee. "I have it on good authority that Agent Rosenthal was stirring the pot about a variety of things, one being a wave of apparently random bombings throughout California that seem to have no distinct connection."

Joe glanced at the head of the group. "Cooper and I discussed it last night. The only tie I can come up with is patriotism. Law enforcement, military,"—he ticked them off on his fingers—"veterans, first responders. They keep the law, fight for our country, help those in need. They're always strong targets for terrorists, whether homegrown or foreign."

That earned him several nods.

Bobby broke his cookie in two and dunked half in his coffee before taking a bite. "Let's assume Kendrick tampered with the report. We still don't understand why, and we're hoping you can give us some ideas. Was she trying to cover her butt since Sam had reported suspicions about the Aztec bomber before it happened and Kendrick didn't take it seriously? Or in order to throw suspicion on Samantha?"

"Suspicion that she was behind the Aztec bombing?" Joe shook his head. "I'm not sure where you're going with this."

Ronni turned her hands palms up. "Why else would Kendrick try to make Agent Rosenthal look like a terrorist? Was she undermining Rosenthal's expertise to give her a reason to ignore that report? Or was it something deeper?"

Joe needed to watch his words carefully. He owed no loyalty to Alison, but he also had no proof she'd set Sam up.

Plus, he was on the verge of defending Sam and blowing the idea he didn't care about her. If he slipped and let the task-force know he still loved their most-wanted, he'd be yanked off this case before he could blink. "I knew Alison for a brief time, and we didn't get along, so I can't tell you how her mind works. I can make assumptions, but that doesn't provide evidence, and that's what we need to confirm these theories."

Another exchange of looks. They wanted to trust him, and they respected the fact he wasn't bad mouthing his former boss, but they knew he was holding back.

Cooper met his gaze head on. "We're doing what we do best —brainstorming. If we have a chance in hell of figuring out where Samantha Rosenthal is, and if she's guilty of the Independence Day bombing, we have to go down a whole lot of theoretical roads. Like I said, what's discussed here, stays here. Anything you say remains between us. I'm not looking for proof or evidence right now. What I need are ideas and possibilities, no matter how crazy, and we can't come up with those, unless we understand exactly who we're dealing with."

Bobby finished his cookie and brushed crumbs from his hands. "I tried tracing Rosenthal and Kendrick to the other bombers and found no obvious connections, other than Rosenthal's report. But, there were two interesting things that did come up. All of the agents assigned to investigate the bombings, at some point, had worked with or under Kendrick. The other thing they all have in common is Kyle Dunmire. I don't suppose he told you who he reported to on a weekly basis?"

"No, but I have the feeling you're going to tell me it was

Alison."

Bobby pointed a finger at Joe to let him know he was correct. "Up until she was fired, Kendrick was Kyle's direct contact. He didn't know her by name, from what I've gathered, only submitted the analysis reports directly to a special inbox that she controlled."

"Why her?" Joe asked.

"She had a coding background and understood the program. Two years ago, she was on the committee that oversees the Quiet Streets project, because she had the history of building databases and coding software."

Joe heard Sam make a noise, suggesting this revelation made total sense to her. "So you believe there's a link between Kyle, Alison, and Sam, beyond the fact she was Sam's boss, and Kyle's to a certain extent?"

Ronni did a half-eye roll and snorted. "You can quit playing dumb, Joe. Who do you think killed Kyle?"

He sat back and blew out a deep breath. Playing dumb had never worked for him. "It's not Alison. I almost wish it was, but according to the handful of facts I've discovered, there could be a mystery woman, who doesn't match Alison's description, and may be responsible."

They all looked pleased he'd finally divulged one of his secrets. "Any idea who this woman is?" Cooper asked.

Joe shook his head, hearing Sam in his ear, giving him the riot act for sharing the information. "No, but I intend to find out."

He checked his watch, and stood. "I'm on my way to meet someone I believe could be important to this case. Thank you for dinner," he said to Celina. "I'll check in tomorrow if I find out anything."

He glanced at Bobby. "Keep digging. You're on the right trail."

And with that cryptic mic drop, he let himself out.

18

———

The parking lot of the sports bar was gravel, an assortment of vehicles casting long shadows here and there under the sparse solar lights.

Heat lightning flashed to the west, a storm rolling in off the ocean. The temperature had dropped at least ten degrees and Sam was grateful. The couple hours in the car at Harris' had nearly killed her, the sun still up, and very little air moving.

Joe cruised the parking lot and Sam pointed to where a narrow access drive lead to the back. "There," she said. "Let's make sure we find a spot where your car is out of sight but I can still see the front entrance."

The headlights illuminated the side of the building as they drove to the back. Here, it was darker, the single light above the rear exit throwing a sickly glow on a beat-up dumpster and a black pickup that had seen better days.

The truck probably belonged to the owner. Two cars sat hidden in the shadows, and Sam assumed these belonged to staff members.

Joe found a spot off to the side in the sand under a scraggly tree that was perfect. She could see the front lot with ease and most of the entrance. If she leaned far enough to the right, she could still see the rear of the place as well.

"Don't let her touch you or give you anything," she told him.

He checked his reflection in the mirror, then looked down his shirt to the hidden wire. "Are you jealous, Rosenthal?"

She didn't want him anywhere near Alison, but she wasn't going to let him know that. "GPS sensors can be small enough to stick on a business card or slip into a pocket. Trust me, she's devious enough to use one to track you."

He leaned across the seat to kiss her. "I promise I won't let her get within a foot of me."

That made her inordinately happy. "Fair warning...if you flirt to try to get information out of her, I'll probably lose my shit."

He grinned. "Thanks for the heads up. I may have to lead her on a bit to get her to open up, but I promise no overt flirting."

Alison had to be behind the setup, Sam was sure of it, and Joe was probably the only person who could get her to lower her guard, if he could convince her he was hunting Sam.

She kissed him back and watched as he took the keys from the ignition. "Could you leave them this time? That way I can run the air when I get hot."

He stretched his long body out of the car and leaned down to look at her. "No dice."

"Why not?" At the smile he gave her, understanding dawned. "You don't trust me."

"Only in so far as you might take off and try to fix this on your own. We're a team now, and whatever happens, we do this together, every step of the way. Got it?"

"Yeah, I got it. I'm not going to take off. I promise."

That didn't seem to appease him. He strolled away, pocketing the keys, and went to the front of the bar without a glance back.

As she watched him enter, she said a few expletives under her breath. "Just testing your wire," she told him.

He chuckled, and she heard the muted sounds of the bar filtering into the microphone. The rise and fall of laughter and conversations, the clinking of plates and silverware. A hostess greeted Joe and asked if he was meeting someone. A moment later he must have been seated. "She's not here yet. I'm in a booth on the east side."

She pictured the layout of the interior and where he was. "Are you facing the entrance?"

"Yes, ma'am."

"Do you see anyone suspicious? Anyone watching you?"

"Nope." The waitress arrived, and Joe ordered a drink. After she left, he resumed filling Sam in. "It's not that busy, so I should be able to keep an eye on everyone."

They'd discussed their plan of action before arriving. Alison wasn't one to work alone, and if she suspected Joe was pumping her for information, she'd have somebody in the bar already. Sam knew he was using his phone as a prop while he murmured things to her, in case anyone was watching. He would look like he was talking on it.

A sleek red convertible pulled in the front lot. "Here we go," Sam said. "She's still driving that Jaguar she had when she worked for the Bureau."

"A zebra can't change its stripes," Joe said.

"More like a cougar."

She parked away from the other vehicles, most likely to avoid getting any dings in her baby. She stepped out, adjusting her tight skirt and flipping her hair over her shoulder. Her gaze scanned the parking lot, and Sam slid low in the seat. She was certain Alison couldn't see her inside Joe's car, thanks to the shadows, but she wasn't taking chances.

Alison reached for her purse, closed the door and locked it. One more scan before she stalked across the gravel. Sam envied the way she kept her balance on three-inch heels, and hated her a little more for always being so put together and stylish.

Another flash of lightning illuminated the sky, making Sam jump. "Show time," she said.

Once inside, Alison found and greeted Joe and the two of them discussed frivolous things like the heat. The waitress returned with Joe's drink and Alison's order.

Sam climbed into the backseat, gritting her teeth at the sound of the woman's voice, and the meaningless chit chat. If they didn't get to business soon, she was going to pull her hair out.

Needing a distraction, she raised the cushion.

Joe was another zebra who couldn't change his stripes. He always had this hidden spot in his car to carry his tools of the trade. Bottled water, food, stun guns, handcuffs, and weapons were stashed inside.

The headlights of cars pulling in and leaving flashed around, mixing with the lightning as she inventoried the contents.

Shoving the jerky strips away, she grabbed two protein bars, some hollow points, a flak vest, and hand sanitizer. She felt like she needed to dump it all over her, listening to Alison's purring voice as she asked questions of Joe concerning his new job as a bounty hunter. "It must be so exciting," she crooned.

Sam held an imaginary gun to her head and set it off, rolling her eyes at the same time.

Sweat beaded on her brow as she considered this new relationship with Joe. She'd fallen for him all over again. Not that she'd ever gotten over him to begin with, but this felt different.

The teasing was the same, the competition, too. Maybe because this time she had no one else to lean on, and no matter how independent she thought she was, she needed him.

She liked Tasers, so she took the one hidden in the box,

along with a GPS tracker. Inventory complete, she opened a protein bar and went back to watching the lot.

Aggravation at Alison burned through her, making her contemplate putting it on the woman's car. If Alison didn't give up anything tonight—and Sam sincerely doubted she would—at least they could track her movements, and figure out if there was any possibility she was indeed part of this.

An older model Buick wheeled in up front. Slowly, it drove among the parked cars and made its way toward the side. Headlights flashed into the interior of Joe's vehicle.

Sam ducked, heart racing, and stayed hidden until she heard the crunch of gravel as the Buick pulled into the rear lot. It was probably a second-shift staff member, or maybe a couple looking for a private place to make out.

The car circled the lot and came back around, passing Joe's Beemer once more. When the sound of the wheels grew faint, Sam popped her head up and saw it make its way to a spot far from the bar entrance.

It appeared there was a couple in the front seat. No one got out for several long moments, and Sam went back to finishing the protein bar. She dug a soda from the cooler and popped the lid. As she drank, she saw a woman emerge from the passenger side.

Recognition hit and she nearly dropped the soda.

It was Kyle's neighbor.

The gal briefly scanned the lot and started across it, heading in Sam's direction. "Shit."

Joe paused in what he was saying to Alison. He couldn't exactly reply without giving away the fact they were in communication, and she rushed to explain. "No worries. It's just Kyle's neighbor. That girl I spoke to the other night. She must've seen your car and recognized it. She's headed this way."

She knew he was mentally asking why. "She's got a flashlight...aww, hell, she's probably figured out who I am and thinks she can find me and get the bounty money."

Sam stuck the open soda in a cup holder and quickly crawled inside Joe's supply box, pulling the seat back in place, but leaving a slight crack so she could see out. The compartment was too small with all the stuff Joe had in it, but there was no other hiding place except the trunk, and no time to get in there.

Kyle's neighbor had a Bluetooth in her ear and used the flashlight to scan the interior. Sam saw her walk toward the back, as she circled the rear, sending a beam into the backseat, then the front. The girl leaned down and looked under the car.

When she straightened, she shone the light into the nearby palms, and over the dumpster.

"Samantha?" she called. "Hey, if you're out here, I just want you to know, I don't mean any harm. My uncle wants to talk to you. And, by the way, I'm unarmed."

Sam could only see her back as the gal leaned on the hood. She saw her raise her hands in the air, in case Sam was watching.

Who the hell was her uncle? And why did he want to talk to her?

The girl sat there for a good five minutes, and in her ear, Sam heard Joe excuse himself from the table to use the restroom. To her, he said, "What the hell is going on?"

She kept her voice a whisper. "Nothing. Stay with Alison. I can handle this."

The girl bent at the front and didn't reappear for a long moment. What was she doing?

Sam heard a *thunk*—a magnetic sound. Was she putting a tracker on Joe's vehicle?

When she rose, she said into the Bluetooth, "No sign of her." There was a pause. "Of course, I checked underneath. I know how to do my job."

What the...?

"I'm going in. She could be there in disguise. Besides I'm hungry. You want anything?"

She walked away and disappeared into the bar.

Joe was chattering in her ear again, telling her he was coming out.

"She's in there with you," Sam told him. "She's definitely looking for me, but I don't know why. She said something about her uncle wanting to talk to me. Maybe you should accidentally run into her and ask some questions about why she's here."

"I don't like this," he said.

"Me either, but it might be fun to pit her and Alison against each other if they're both after me."

Her attempt to lighten the situation went over like a lead ball. "We should pull the plug on this operation."

"You haven't even asked Alison anything pertinent yet. Joe, this is our chance. You're probably the only person who can get past her armor."

She heard a heavy sigh. "All right. Stay in the car. I'll see what I can do, but if anything else happens, I'm out of here. *We're* out of here."

"I'm fine," Sam insisted. "This girl is an amateur. We can handle her. It's Alison we have to be careful with."

Sam slowly slipped out of the compartment, staying hidden from anyone who might be looking her direction.

The night was dark, clouds obscuring any light from the moon and stars. As she peered over the seats and dash, she could see the man in the Buick had his driver's window down, his hand flicking a cigarette to get rid of the ashes. Was this the uncle?

Had to be. She couldn't see his face as it was hidden by shadows. Sam stroked the Taser and decided the tracking device had a new purpose. Carefully opening the rear passenger door, she slipped into the sandy gravel.

The opposite side of the sports bar gave her cover to move to the front lot, where she clung to the deep shadows as she went from vehicle to vehicle. She was closing in on the Buick.

The man had backed into a space near a palm tree and away from the lights. She slowly crept forward.

Her heart raced and she forced it to slow down, her breathing to even out. Alison was the big fish here, but she wanted to know who this man was, and why he wanted to talk to her.

She guessed he might be a bounty hunter, like Joe, or someone looking to score the reward money on her. Either way, the girl was trained enough to help him.

Figures, Sam thought. She continued into a mess of scrub brush directly behind the car and sat there for a moment, deciding whether she was really going to risk this.

Convinced she needed more intel on these two, she was about to sneak forward to reach the underside of the trunk, when she heard him say, "I told you, don't let Cahill see you."

Sam's heart jumped into her throat, at first thinking he was talking to her, but then she realized he was speaking to the girl once again.

His voice was hoarse, as if he had laryngitis. "I mean it, Sorscha. Alison either. She'll have a fit."

Alison! She *was* in on this. Of course.

Kyle's neighbor was a plant. But why? And how long had this Sorscha been keeping tabs on the guy? Was the 'uncle' in the car the male neighbor she'd met that night who'd pretended to be Sorscha's boyfriend?

Joe had recommenced his discussion with Alison, but Sam's mind was spinning, not listening to them. She crept forward and ever so gently attached the tracker as the man continued to lecture Sorscha on being careful. At closer range, she thought he sounded almost familiar.

Slipping back into the scrub brush, she silently released the breath she'd been holding and regained her composure. After a moment, she stayed bent at the waist as she hurried past the other cars toward the shadows on the far side of the building.

Unexpectedly, she heard Joe in her ear demanding her attention. "Sam! What are you doing? What's going on?"

"Why aren't you talking to Alison?" she hissed quietly, slowing.

"I'm at the bar getting her a drink. Talk to me."

"The girl and her uncle are apparently working with Alison. I'm not sure who he is, but it's possible he was posing as a college co-ed the other night. He's got a cold or something, so I don't recognize his voice. None of this makes sense, but he mentioned Alison's name. She *is* behind this, and she had them watching Kyle's."

"I told you to stay in the car. Look, we can figure out who those two are and why they're pretending to be students later. It's too dangerous, we're not messing with them, or Alison, any longer tonight."

"Okay," she agreed. This new wrinkle was something she needed to think about. "I'm heading back to your car."

"Good." She heard the relief in his voice. Glancing over her shoulder to make sure the man in the car hadn't moved, she was relieved to see he was too busy smoking to notice her.

"I'm going to take Alison her drink, then I'm coming out," Joe said.

Lightning flashed, closer now, and illuminated the man's face. Sam sucked in a breath.

What the...? *Holy shit.*

Rushing along the rear, heading for the shadows that would take her to Joe's car.

It couldn't be. Not him.

Her thoughts were too tangled, a dozen different pieces of the puzzle beginning to fall into place. As she crouched to scoot up to the passenger side of Joe's car, she heard the crunch of gravel behind her and whirled.

Holy shit was right.

Sorscha stood there, smiling, a gun in her hand. "Well, hello there."

She raised it and aimed right at Sam.

Joe set Alison's drink on the table. He was done with this.

"I don't know what game you're playing," he said to the woman seated in the booth looking innocent, "but I'm not participating."

She opened her red lipsticked mouth to say something, her brows squeezing together in a frown, but in his ear he heard Sam say "I'm in trouble, Joe."

Everything in him froze.

He didn't wait for Alison's response. "Don't move. I'm on my way."

He jetted for the door, impatiently weaving through the growing crowd. A waitress carrying a tray of beers stepped in front of him and he barely missed her, shifting to his left...and into the path of a patron.

The young, preppy-looking kid jumped at the same time and knocked into her, sending her and the tray flying.

A table of two couples ended up wearing the beer, the crash of breaking glass cutting through the din. Shouts rang out. Joe didn't wait, and jetting for the door once more.

A hand seized one of his arms, and he found it attached to a half-drunk bald guy who'd been at the bar. "Seems like you've got some cleaning up to do, son," the guy said.

Get to Sam. Get to Sam.

Instinct took hold. Joe slugged the guy in the gut. Not hard enough to hurt, but it made the bozo release his grip.

Two steps forward, and Joe realized he had the entire bar's attention. People yelled, "stop him!" More volunteers rising to their feet to give chase.

Another hand landed on his forearm and he wheeled to punch whoever it was, but found himself looking into the face of Alison. "Joe, what the hell? What's going on?"

He had no intention of answering, and as various men started to close in, he shoved her away. Turning for the door again, he heard a sound that made his blood run cold.

Bam!

His ear exploded with the noise.

Gun.

Sam!

Bolting forward, he was tackled by two older guys, who looked like they'd been Marines in their day. He jerked out of their grips, and heard Alison shout from behind him, "He's a federal agent. Let him go."

Why was she lying on his behalf? No time to speculate, and the Marines backed down.

The bouncer had taken up residence at the entrance, a massive roadblock. Unmoving, he offered a blank expression, and stood casually with his hands interlaced.

The guy's black skin gleamed under the bar's lights. As Joe rushed forward, the bouncer smiled, revealing a missing tooth. Three hundred pounds, Joe estimated. Most of it muscle.

Without warning, a younger version of the veteran Marines leaped in his way and took a swing.

Joe dodged left, the blow grazing his shoulder. He used the guy's momentum to spin him off, into another table.

People gasped and shouted. The bouncer continued to smile, blocking his way to Sam.

Alison come up behind him, shouting at the bouncer. "Get out of the way, moron!"

A losing proposition to go head to head with the guy, but he'd taken down similar sized men, on the run and who had nothing to lose. The trick was to outsmart them, not try to outfight them.

Joe's pulse beat a hard tempo, his drive to get to Sam overwhelming everything else. "You have a federal fugitive in your parking lot," he told the guy, resurrecting his FBI persona. "Get out of the way or I'll hold you and this bar responsible for letting her escape. You'll find your ass in prison for the next ten years."

Smiley grinned harder and stepped forward. "Is that so?"

Joe threw a punch at the guy's face. As he attempted to deflect it and dodge out of the way, Joe raised a booted foot and kicked him in the gut. The big man hardly budged, but Joe followed that up with a second kick to the knee.

Bone snapped and the bouncer nosedived into the hostess station, knocking it over and scattering the woman standing there.

Joe hit the door and flew onto the bar's wooden front porch, scrambling to the end closest to the gravel drive on the side.

Just as he vaulted the railing, he heard Alison call. "Joe! Wait!"

Landing on the gravel, he found himself spotlighted by car's headlights. It sped by, nearly running him over. The front bumper nicked him as he lunged out of the way, his shoulder slamming into the side of the building.

Ricocheting off, Joe landed on hands and knees. Gravel dug into his palms, but he didn't feel it. Adrenaline pumped hard in his veins. Fear chased it. Bounding up, he ran for his BMW, calling Sam's name at the top of his lungs.

As he skidded to a stop next to the car, the darkness was thick, the silence of the night heavy back here. The sickly light from the rear exit barely illuminated anything, but he caught sight of disturbed gravel.

A struggle. He could see it. His already tense belly cramped hard. Jerking out his cell, he turned on the flashlight and shone it around, stopping when he found a puddle of dark liquid soaking into the gravel.

He crouched down and touched it. Blood.

Sam's blood.

Alison ran up behind him, having removed her heels. "Holy hell," she said, eyeing dark liquid. "What happened?"

He rounded on her, but then looked toward the bar's front parking lot. "Who the fuck was that?"

"In the car? No idea. Some drunk?"

Behind the Beemer's trunk, something glinted in the grass. He found Sam's burner phone lying there. Snatching it up, he yanked the driver's door open.

As he jammed the keys in the ignition, the passenger side flew open and Alison slid in.

"Get the hell out of my car. Now!"

"They took a right," she said, pointing toward the main road. When he didn't move, she waved the finger. "What are you waiting for? Go!"

He didn't have time to argue. Sam's life was on the line. Growling under his breath, he shoved the car into drive, gravel spraying as he put his foot on the gas and took off.

20

______

Sam was in a fog. Sounds came as if far away—
footsteps, low murmuring, crying.

Her tongue and throat burned, the tingle of chloroform in
her nose. She swallowed hard and peeled her eyes open a few
centimeters, seeing a dirty wooden floor her head was
laying on.

For several seconds, she floated in the fog, allowing the rest
of her senses to come online. Heat, sweat, a dustiness and
empty echoes filtered in.

"She's awake," a female voice said.

The sound was still so distant, and as Sam craned her neck
to try and glance in that direction, sharp pains shot through her
body.

Her hands were secured behind her, the arm she was lying
on stinging with pins and needles from lack of blood flow. Her
left leg burned, radiating lances of white-hot agony from her
knee.

Sorscha came into view, kneeling and looking her over.
"Good, we can wrap this up."

Sam tried to spit out a curse, but her mouth and tongue

wouldn't obey. Rage burned in her belly and she manage to grunt, "You shot me!"

The woman grinned. "Couldn't let you run, now, could I?"

Someone had wrapped Sam's knee, and along with assessing the rest of her aches and pains, she realized the normal weight of the earbud was gone.

Bad news. She had no way to contact Joe now.

The sobbing increased, drawing her attention past her feet. The room was nearly devoid of furniture. A single, cheap floor lamp lit the space. Beyond where she lay, a woman was tied to a chair, duct tape over her mouth.

As more brain cells fired, Sam forgot the pain, the bitter taste on her tongue. Anxiety racked her and she struggled to sit up. Her head was too woozy, and vertigo sent her to the floor again. "Hetty?"

Her voice came out strange, ragged. Hetty let go another strangled cry.

Sorscha had shot her, and her so-called 'uncle' had chloroformed Sam after he'd wheeled up in his car.

She'd been on her knees at that point, thanks to the bullet that had grazed her left one, and Sorscha had stepped forward and tased her.

Bitch.

Sam had fallen over in the gravel, and Frank had jumped out to throw her in the backseat. Sorscha had vaulted into his spot and they'd taken off like a bat outta hell.

Paralyzed, Sam couldn't fight Frank and the chloroform, but she remembered her boss's face hovering over hers with a sad smile.

Her rotten luck—not only had Alison been the worst of the worst, Sam now realized Frank was too.

Her boss. He'd betrayed her.

Even now, her mind bent and tried to wrap around that fact.

Now, he came into view, staring down at her. "Sorry about this, Samantha."

Sorry? "How could you?" Glancing around urgently, she attempted to figure out where they were, how Frank had gotten Hetty. "You know I didn't bomb that parade."

"Oh, I know, but you're too damn smart for your own good."

The room, while nearly empty, reminded her of another she'd been in recently. The layout of the door, the windows, the smell.

Kyle's.

But this wasn't his apartment. She saw a worn wooden staircase to the right. Next to it, an entryway that led to a kitchen.

Sorscha leaned against the frame there. "How do you want to lay it out?"

Frank swiveled to look at a spot behind Sam. It took everything she had to follow his gaze, rolling herself over on to her cuffed hands. Sharp pain ran up her arms, but her stomach bottomed out when she saw Dec in a similar chair and position as Hetty.

While Hetty cried, Dec glanced at Sam with wild eyes. He was trying to say something, but the duct tape over his mouth blocked it. He rocked, exerting himself to move closer, and Sam whispered, "Oh god, Dec. I'm so, so sorry. Hetty…"

Frank, with his slight build, and short graying hair, came more fully into view as he walked to a dilapidated coffee table and hefted the bat lying there.

Dec's weapon of choice.

Frank turned in a lazy circle, keen eyes glancing at Sorscha, Sam, then the others. "We have to make it seem as if she was living here, in this lower part of the duplex."

His gaze went to the door, flicked to Sam, as he spoke to his supposed niece. "These two,"—he used the bat to point to Hetty and Dec—"were staying here with her. You notified me you saw her, so I came to talk Samantha into turning herself in.

There was a gunfight. Sam and her friends were killed, but they managed to knock over a candle, which started a fire, and bye-bye evidence."

"But I'll get the reward, right?" Sorscha asked.

"You can't do this," Sam pleaded. "Please, Frank. I don't know how you got involved in all of this, but we'll work together and figure it out. Let Dec and Hetty go—they haven't done anything. They don't even know who I really am."

He gave her that sad smile. "Wish it was that easy, kid. You really were a good agent."

"Why?" She hoisted herself into a half-sitting position. Her head swam, the bitterness on her tongue making her want to gag. "Why are you doing this? Are you the one who set me up?"

He twirled the bat in his hand. "I didn't start it, but you know how it is when you love someone—you'll do anything for them. Kinda like Cahill putting his life on the line for you."

Love? What the hell was he talking about? "Who are you covering for?" But as soon as Sam asked, understanding dawned. "Tell me it's not Alison."

"Crazy woman. She got under my skin. This plan was concocted years ago—I honestly thought we were just making stuff up. Thinking about different scenarios to help her climb the ranks. You know, playing 'what if' while we were both stationed in Bumblefuck, Arkansas."

He looked serene for a moment, as if remembering happier times. "She felt completely unappreciated, and simply wanted somebody in the Bureau to recognize her talents. Guess I never thought she'd actually carry out any of these ideas."

"What ideas? The bombings?"

"She's mental." He made a twirling motion near his temple with one finger, then looked at Sam as if she would understand. "Adamant she wanted fame. She screwed up, and then you started figuring things out. Downward spiral from there.

Instead of accomplishing a big win and having the Bureau reward her for it, she ended up fired because of you."

"She did that to herself. If she'd done her job—"

He gripped the bat and swung it in an arc in the air as if taking a swing at a ball. "With this, I'll get her reinstated. Things will go back to the way they were, and she'll get that promotion she wanted. I'll have helped her attain the fame she so desperately craves."

Oh my god. Alison was worse than Sam had anticipated. And Frank? He knew the bitch was crazy and was willing to kill to help her.

Throat tight, her mind raced with ways to get out of this— or at least Hetty and Dec. They were her first concern. Then Joe. *Keep him talking.* "And Kyle? Why kill him?"

Frank glanced at Sorscha. The girl still stood in the doorway to the kitchen, acting as if this was all commonplace. Just an average day in her life.

"You," Sam snarled. "You lied to me. Alison was the woman Kyle fell for. You purposely misled me about that, didn't you?"

Sorscha grinned. "It was too easy. Frank told me you were this really smart FBI agent, and I totally fooled you. That night, when you rode your bike here? I didn't know then who you were, but I made sure I put a tracker on the bike, cause I knew you must be mixed up with all of this..." She motioned at the group. "You didn't even realize it, did you?"

In that moment, Sam hated her even more than she did Alison. Maybe herself a little, too, for letting this amateur get the best of her.

"We have plenty of evidence to show Cahill's been helping you," Frank said.

"We even have pictures," Sorscha added. "Such a shame to get rid of him. He's tasty looking."

A string of curses left her lips, as she mentally kicked herself. All this time, she thought she'd been doing such a good job at hiding, keeping Joe safe, Hetty and Dec, too. What the hell was she going to do now?

Play the game. There was nothing else to do.

She raised her chin, eyeing Frank. First, she'd try reasoning with him, although she doubted it was worth the breath. "Let Joe go. Them too." She jerked her head at Hetty and Dec. "Do whatever you want to me, but you can't kill all of us and pretend it's an accident. Internal affairs will investigate. The SCVC has already put together many of the pieces. They'll figure out the rest. You'll be exposed, Alison will go down, and you'll have our deaths on your head. She isn't worth it, Frank. You're looking at life in prison."

He extracted a digital recorder from his pocket and held it up. "If you confess to being the one behind the bombings, clearing Alison of them, I'll consider not killing Cahill. But the rest of them...?"

He let the threat hang in the air.

Sam knew he wouldn't leave Joe alone. Joe could out him *and* Alison. But what could she do? She had to try something to save the man she loved.

An image of her dad rose in her mind—he'd died a hero and here she was about to die a fugitive. Not only that, because of her blunders, she was about to get the three people in the world who had stood by her killed.

Her bloody knee, wrapped in an old t-shirt, throbbed. Her head did too. Hetty continued to cry softly, Dec was making noises in the back of his throat, as if trying to get her to glance at him. When she did, she saw the word "no" in his eyes.

Don't do it. Joe wouldn't want her to confess to anything, no matter what Frank promised. He was just as crazy as Alison, and she couldn't trust him or Sorscha.

She prayed Joe would realize she'd placed a tracker on Frank's car at the restaurant. Maybe he was on the way. He wouldn't be here in time to stop what was about to happen, but he would catch Frank in the act and the man wouldn't get away with it.

Frank set the device on the table. He tapped the bat against his leg. "Do we have a deal, Samantha? Your confession for Cahill's life?"

She raised her chin again, narrowing her eyes. "How about this?" she countered. "You take that recorder and shove it up your ass, and I won't kill you or your niece in the next few minutes."

Sorscha barked an indignant laugh, but Frank eyed her sullenly.

He glanced around at the interior. "Okay, then, here's how we're going to stage this."

Moving to Dec, he motioned at Sorscha. She walked past Sam, kicking her in the foot.

"Your junkie friend attacked Sorscha," Frank explained to Sam. Then he looked at his niece. "You ready?"

Sorscha braced herself. "Do it."

Frank swung the bat, nailing her in the upper thigh and she yelped. Rubbing the spot, she said through gritted teeth, "That's gonna leave a bruise."

"That's the idea." Frank faced Dec and everything in Sam propelled her to get up. Before she could, Frank reared back, the bat held high. "But being the junkie that he is, Sorscha easily overwhelmed him."

Dec's already wide eyes turned alarmed.

Sam screamed, "No!"

Frank nailed him in the temple with a sickening *thud*.

Dec toppled sideways, chair and all. From behind her duct tape, Hetty screamed.

Sam lunged, but her knee wouldn't hold and Sorscha struck her, knocking her away. She fell to the ground, everything screaming in pain once more.

"Next." Frank moved to Hetty. Her screaming stopped, and

her chest rose and fell, hyperventilating. The small woman, rocked, gaze jerking between Frank, the bat, and Sam.

"Don't you dare," Sam growled, wrestling against her failing knee. "I will kill you!"

"This gal tried to run." Frank handed off the bat to Sorscha. From his back beltline, he pulled a handgun. "She almost made it to the door, too. So I had to shoot her."

Frank walked behind Hetty, as Sam threw herself forward. "Nooo!"

Too late. He fired a bullet into Hetty's back.

Sam screamed.

21

———

Joe raced down the freeway. His focus jumped between the pulsing red circle on the map on his phone, Alison in the seat next to him, and the traffic.

Sam and her damn spy shit. It'd taken him nearly a mile to realize his phone was pulsing, and when he'd pulled it out, the app for a GPS tracker blinked like Rudolph's nose.

She'd managed to place a device on the car of her kidnappers. For that, he wanted to kiss her. He'd used them on rare occasions when chasing a fugitive, but this had taken his love of them to a whole new level.

"Where are we heading?" Alison asked, squinting at the map.

Toward the outskirts of the university, from the looks of it. The kidnappers had stopped, in fact, right in Kyle's neighborhood.

He'd already be on their ass, if not for a multi-car pileup that had cost him nearly fifteen minutes and a detour.

He sped around a car, then took an offramp. "You have no idea who has Sam?" he demanded for the third time.

"I told you, none. I can't believe you're actually dumb enough to be helping her. She probably got picked off by another bounty hunter, or some nutcase who saw her in the parking lot and figured out who she was. Her picture is all over everything."

Joe thought about shooting Alison and dumping her body, but he didn't want to waste more time. "I don't believe you."

Although he was focused on merging into traffic, he didn't miss her eyeroll. "Get over it, Cahill. You've now implicated me in this, and if we *do* catch up to her, I might even cheer for her kidnapper. If nothing else, I'm claiming the reward."

He passed a large RV, receiving blaring horns for his trouble. "You'll be lucky if I don't kill you and dispose of your body before the night's over."

She snorted but fell silent.

Fine with him. As he weaved through suburbia, thankfully less congested than the freeway at this time of night, he sent SOS texts to his brothers, as well as Cooper Harris. Brief and to the point, forwarding the location of Kyle's.

As he cruised to a stop a block down from the apartment building, he saw the neighbors' place was dark.

"You need to get closer so we can see what's going on," Alison chided.

"*We* aren't doing anything," he shot back. "You're staying here. I'm going in."

"You don't even know who's in there or what they're planning." She pointed out her window. "There's an alley behind these houses. Park there, and come up to the duplex from the rear."

How did she know about the alley?

Joe eased a few yards closer, bringing the lower apartment into view. A dark Buick, nearly hidden behind the hedgerow, was tucked up tight to the side of the house. The faintest of lights crept out the edges of the first floor windows. Was someone downstairs?

No light upstairs, so whoever had Sam, was indeed, in the lower apartment.

Joe once again parked, debating his options.

"You can't walk up to the front door." Alison shook her head. "I mean, if this *is* a bounty hunter, why bring her here? Something about this is off."

The sick feeling in Joe's stomach told him why. "They're going to kill her." He reached for his door, pocketing his phone. He needed to get his gear on, arm himself. "Stay. Here."

As he exited, Alison said, "Not on your life." She bailed out and looked at him over the roof. "You're too emotional about this and you don't know what you're walking in to. You need backup, and I'm all you've got."

He considered hitting her with the stun gun, at least that'd shut her up. Then something caught his eye.

There was the faint sound of a bass drum, music. The neighbors.

He thought about the girl who talked to Sam, telling them about Kyle's girlfriend. The one who'd been at the bar tonight.

The woman the neighbor had described as Kyle's girlfriend was Alison's opposite in every way. And yet...

Acting as though he were going to actually let her play backup, he went to his trunk and popped it. "What's your poison?" he asked.

As expected, she followed, and peered inside, admiring the weapons stashed there. As she did so, he grabbed a Taser and looked it over. "How did you know about the alley, by the way? You can't see it from here."

In a split second, her gaze swung to his, and before she could run, he zapped her.

22

Sorscha kicked her again, this time in her damaged knee. Horror and rage burned in Sam's throat, and it was all she could do not to vomit.

She inch-wormed to Hetty, who now lay on the ground, eyes distant as blood stained her shirt. Drip by drip, it began to pool on the floor.

But she was still breathing. "Hang on, Hetty," she whispered. Tears streaked down her face. "Hang on."

"And now for you." Frank yanked her up, shoving her against the stairs. Sam's knee screamed and gave out, but Sorscha pinned her to the wooden railing.

The house was old and hadn't been taken care of since it'd been split into apartments. The spindles wobbled at the pressure.

"You gonna shoot me in the back, too?" Sam spit at Frank. "Coward."

Her goading didn't seem to matter to him. He and Sorscha simply exchanged a glance, as if the game was getting old.

Think, Sam demanded her brain. She needed to clear her emotions and do something.

Gritting her teeth against the pain in her knee, she glared at both of them. "Traitors to your country and cowards on top of it."

Sorscha gave her a shove and the railing shuddered. "Shut up, already," the girl sneered. To her uncle, she said, "I've got her. Go ahead."

I will not die like this. She wouldn't let Alison and Frank get away with what they'd done.

Cold fury burned in her veins. As she sensed Frank raise the gun, she gathered her strength and slammed into Sorscha.

Bam. The gun went off, a bullet whizzing past her ear close enough to raise her hair.

Sam dropped to the floor. Sorscha cried, toppling sideways and reaching for the railing.

Another shot rang out, but Sam had already rolled, using the momentum to knock Sorscha down. Wheeling high up onto her back, she drew her legs in as close as she could and rocked forward sliding the handcuffs over the bottoms of her feet. Her damaged leg refused to obey and the foot caught on the chain of the cuffs, but her momentum helped jerk it free.

Sorscha lunged and Sam swung out, catching her face with the sharp edge of the metal.

"Hold still, you goddamned brat," Frank growled.

Sorscha jerked back, lips feral as she shrieked obscenities. Sam threw her cuffed wrists over her head, using the chain between them to choke the girl.

The cold fury gave her strength and she whipped Sorscha in front of her to act as a shield. "Put down the gun," she demanded to Frank.

Gagging, Sorscha tried slamming her body weight into Sam, but Sam was already against the wall, using it for leverage.

She tightened her hold, Sorscha's fingers digging at the

metal as she coughed and choked. "Drop. It." She gave a squeeze on the cuffs and the girl stopped squirming.

He eyed her warily for a long moment, then lowered the weapon a few inches as he sized up his options. "Damn it, Sorscha."

The chokehold kept her from speaking, and Sam figured her eyes were bugging about now. Then Frank surprised her, raising the gun once more.

Sam realized with some shock, he was ready to sacrifice his niece to get himself out of this. Instincts kicked in hard. She could see it in his calculating eyes—he planned to shoot Sam right through Sorscha.

Body quaking, mind reeling, she was out of options. Closing her eyes, waiting for the hit to come, her body was too weak to attempt to move both her *and* the girl.

"I wouldn't pull that trigger, if I were you," a hard voice said from the kitchen door.

Sam's eyes flew open. Both hers and Frank's heads whipped to look.

Joe.

He was carrying a body in a fireman's hold and had a gun pointed at Frank. He unceremoniously dumped his package on the floor "You heard her. Drop your weapon or I shoot."

Frank's startled eyes glanced at the woman lying on the floor. Alison. His voice was incredulous. "Ally?"

Joe's gaze flicked to Sam. *Hang on*, it told her.

Her arms shook, losing what little strength they still had, and Sorscha began struggling again. Sam willed everything she had into them, forcing the metal chain across Sorscha's neck to cut off her air. Still, she'd lost so much blood. Her good leg trembled, losing its battle to keep her upright. Black dots danced in front of her eyes.

Joe pointed his gun at Alison, speaking to Frank. "Put down the weapon or she dies."

In the distance, the blare of a siren sounded...or maybe her ears were ringing. The dots grew to shadows. *Do not pass out.*

Joe stayed focused on Frank. "It's over," he told him, his voice level. "The FBI knows everything."

Not quite, Sam thought. Neither they nor Joe had any idea what Frank and Alison had done together.

Or did he?

Frank's lips thinned. He sighed, and slowly, inch by inch, lowered his gun in defeat.

Alison stirred. Frank started to take a step toward her, but he hadn't dropped his weapon. Joe yelled, "Drop it! Now!"

The bastard raised the gun. As he did, Sam shoved Sorscha and sent both of them careening into her uncle.

The girl cried out as they fell as one, knocking Frank sideways. The gun fired, a bullet smacking into the wall behind Joe.

The weight of Sam and Sorscha combined was enough to keep Frank pinned. Joe jumped into the fray, knocking Sorscha in the head with the butt of his gun. He brought a knee down on Frank's arm and the man's weapon came loose from his grip.

Sam slid off the pile, shoving herself away. Frank fought Joe, cursing, before Joe managed to clock him square in the jaw. That shut him up, his lashes fluttering before his eyes rolled up in his head.

Dead silence fell. "Sam?" With swift movements, Joe zip tied their ankles and wrists. "Talk to me. Are you hurt?"

"No," she lied. She slid to Hetty, but the dizziness was too much, and sank to her side.

Her ears were fine—the one thing on her poor, tattered body that was—and the siren grew louder until it seemed as if it was there. She knew it was—Joe had called the cavalry.

She held Hetty's hand, grappling to stay conscious as Joe came to her, a key in hand to unlock the cuffs. Her wrists were chafed from the metal, but that was the least of her worries.

"Hey." He gently tugged her into an embrace. "You got yourself into a mess, didn't you?"

She almost laughed, but it took too much effort, so she sank into him, and wished she could stay there forever. Her throat was too tight to speak so she pointed at her friends, both lying motionless on the floor. Tears burned her eyes.

Reading her mind, Joe released her to check their pulses. He yanked off his flak vest, then his shirt to pad Hetty's bullet wound.

People began to rush in and Joe shouted orders, even as he said to Sam, "They're still alive. Ambulance is on its way."

As more people flooded in, taking care of Alison, Frank, and Sorscha, Joe pulled her into his lap, wrapping his arms around her. Sam closed her eyes and gave in to the threatening darkness to tuck herself into his chest.

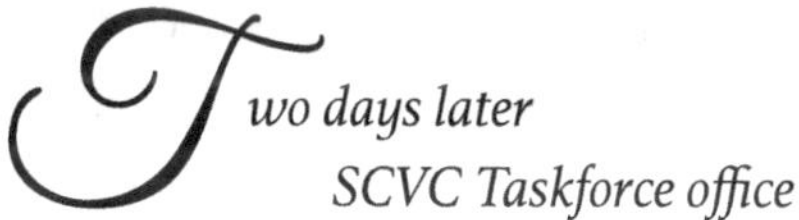

23

*T*wo *days later*
SCVC Taskforce office

SAM LOOKED at the faces staring at her around the meeting table. Dr. Walsh, Cooper Harris, Ronni Punto, Thomas Mann, Director Dupé, and a Special Agent in Charge named Moan from the FBI.

Her left leg was propped on a chair, crutches against the wall behind Joe. He hadn't left her side. She was still tired, battered and bruised, but things were looking up.

"The FBI would like to make an offer concerning your old position," SAC Moan said. He was a slight man, with a balding head and thick eyebrows. They'd flown him in from D.C. to handle the situation, and Sam knew from the look on Dupé's face, he was none too pleased to have Moan stepping in and taking over. "We want you back, and we're prepared to offer a substantial raise with it."

The Bureau was in hot water after releasing the information that had cleared Sam's name and implicated Frank and

Alison in the plot against her. Worse, they were terrorists, and the FBI had two black eyes.

While she'd loved her job, Sam had decided she couldn't go back. Trusting anyone inside the Bureau now was a no-go. "Let me make it clear to everyone," she said, meeting Moan and Dupé's eyes, "I'm not returning."

She sensed Joe having a hard time keeping the smile off his face. He was finally getting what he'd wanted all along—her to get out of undercover work.

She flicked a glare at him. While she wouldn't let him know she was actually relieved to give it up at this point, she didn't want him to think he had the upper hand here. She'd never hear the end of it.

Dr. Walsh leaned forward, tapping a file in front of him. "Since you've been cleared of all charges, and with your field experience, the Domestic Terrorism Taskforce would like to make an official job offer."

And that was a possibility down the road, if she could handle sitting behind a computer. "I'll keep that in mind," she told him. "Thank you for considering me."

Frank, Alison, and Sorscha were in custody. The women were both throwing Frank under the bus, claiming he was the mastermind behind everything and trying to cut a deal with the Justice Department. So far, her former boss had said nothing. He'd lawyered up, and in Sam's eyes, seemed to be taking the fall for those he loved.

She glanced at Joe, wondering how far he'd go because of his love for her. She wasn't sure of her future career, but was one hundred percent ready for a life with the man next to her.

"I definitely plan to continue helping my country." She'd never had any doubt she'd carry on in her parents' footsteps when it came to such. "But you'll understand why I have a bad taste in my mouth at the moment over all this."

Everyone but Harris looked slightly sheepish. He winked at her from the other end.

She and Joe had been invited to his home next weekend for another dinner. In the hospital, Celina had visited and told her about her own encounter with a traitor several years ago. Sam felt an instant bond with the woman, and was looking forward to a potential friendship.

Discussion about closing out the case resumed, the testimony she would provide to the judge, and another job offer, this one from Cooper.

"The taskforce could use someone with your background and skills to help Bobby Dyer." Dyer, his computer guru, i.e., hacker, and good friend. Bobby had been an outstanding agent at one time himself. "We could use intel on the psychology and sociology of terrorists in the field."

Ronni and Thomas often went undercover with gangs and drug cartels, but Sam's experience was a niche, focused on homegrown terrorists. It was an area their group was expanding into, and Cooper and Dupé both wanted an expert such as her to help.

She was definitely interested in that position.

But right now? The only thing she wanted to do was go home and sleep for a week, with Joe on one side, and Jack-Jack on the other. Oh, and to eat. And have sex. And...so many things.

Ronni seemed to understand Sam itched to get done with their meeting. "One more item. I wanted to update you on the social media fundraiser Celina and I put together for your friends. We cracked thirty thousand in donations this morning. The hospital bills will be covered, I promise."

Dec was doing fine after suffering a mild concussion, and Thomas had found a place for him to stay while recuperating. Someone, probably Cooper, had pulled strings at the hospital to keep Dec there the past few days, drying him out and getting him in touch with a therapist. The plan was to help him get back to some type of normal life off the streets.

Hetty was still in serious condition, but she'd pulled through her surgery and the outlook was positive, according to the doctors. It was one day at a time for now, but Sam knew her gritty attitude would help. After her recovery, Sam planned to get her into a special home as well.

"I can't thank you and Celina enough for what you're doing for them," she told Ronni.

Ronni nodded, and Cooper said, "That's what teams do for each other. The taskforce is a family, and I hope one of these days you might join ours, Samantha."

A warm feeling invaded her chest. "I think I'd like that. I just need a little time to feel normal again."

"Take all the time you need," Dupé offered with a smile. "And don't forget to call Olivia. She's been really worried about you."

"I will."

When everything was wrapped up, Joe helped her stand and handed her the crutches. Hating the fact she needed them, Sam hobbled into the bright sunlight of the summer day, welcoming the heat on her face.

Joe had assigned himself as her chauffer, and as he assisted her to his car, Sam saw Caleb and Malachi waiting for them.

Joe's older brothers were twins, all muscles and dark looks, just like him. They'd always given her grief about being too good for Joe, and she'd enjoyed the verbal sparring.

She and Joe stopped in front of them, and Sam said, "Thank you for the other night."

They'd shown up on the heels of an ambulance, and helped get Hetty and Dec headed to the hospital. They'd also kept Joe from making good on his word to kill Alison and Frank, which he'd threatened to do when he'd discovered the extent of her injuries.

Caleb grinned. "Heard you're looking for a new job."

"We've got an opening," Malachi added.

She'd never had so many offers in her life. She'd been contacted by a book publisher and a screenwriter, wanting to tell her story. It was good to have options after her time on the streets with none. "You want me to become a bounty hunter?"

"Fugitive apprehension agent," Joe corrected.

"You've got firsthand experience being a fugitive now," Caleb said with a wink. "You should be able to hunt them down with ease."

Malachi pointed at her leg. "You can answer phones and make coffee until you're on your feet again."

Sam laughed out loud. "In your dreams, boys."

Joe opened the door and guided her in. The Bureau had raised hell, but cleared him of any charges for aiding her, since she was actually not a fugitive, and had brought down the terrorists within their ranks. "Let's go home," he said.

Home for now was the safe house. Since Sam was the hottest topic in the news, reporters had camped out at her place, as well as Joe's.

The drive was long, and Sam fell asleep in the sun coming through her window. When they arrived, Joe once more assisted her and got her up the steps to the door. Inside Jack-Jack greeted her spastically and she found her mom in the kitchen.

They hugged awkwardly around the crutches, and her mom said, "Lunch is ready."

She pointed at the table with two plates of sandwiches and chips.

"Thank you, Mom." Not only had Sam told the taskforce, the feds, and the Justice Department about everything, she'd had to explain all of it to her mother, too. She hoped to never repeat the story again.

Her mother and Joe greeted each other, then Sam received

another hug. "The ring is in the suitcase upstairs with some clothes," she whispered in her ear. "Maybe you should put it back on. Your dad would be so proud."

After she left, Sam sat and devoured the food, Joe smiling as he ate his own and watched. His eyes seemed to eat her up, as well. Jack-Jack begged for scraps, and Joe—the big softie—got the dog a treat from the pantry.

Tired but happy, Sam wondered how she was ever going to thank him for what he'd done. Luckily, she had an idea.

"Can you bring my suitcase down?" she asked.

"Right now?"

She gave him her *pretty please* look. He wiped his hands on a napkin, stood, and kissed the top of her head. "Sure. Be right back."

When he returned, he plopped the bag at her feet and asked, "Is there something inside I can get for you?"

"Nope, I got it." Shuffling through the clothes, she rummaged for the ring. Jack-Jack stuck his nose in to help. Surprisingly—or not—the dog was the one who found the small blue velvet box.

Retrieving it, she slowly opened the lid. Joe smiled expectantly as she took out the ring and held it up between them. "I want to make a deal," she said.

"Okay." He sat back in his chair, amused. "Let's hear it."

"In order to say thank you for risking your career, and your life, for me, I thought I'd make you an offer you can't refuse."

The smile on his face grew. "Is that right?"

She slipped the ring on. "I'll marry you, if we can keep this house and the dog."

He looked as if he were waiting for more. "That's the best you got?"

She nearly threw her plate at him. "It's a damn good deal!"

Joe rose, scratching his chin and looking as though he needed to think it over. He came to her side of the table, hauled her up, and held her there as he gazed down into her eyes. "This was the house I planned to give you," he said, his voice ragged with emotion. "Your mom and I kept it a secret so you wouldn't know anything about it until our wedding night. It was a safe house for her and your dad if they ever needed it. She sold it to me."

Her heart tapped danced in her chest. "You mean we can stay here? This is *ours*?"

He leaned down and touched her nose with his. "Only if you marry me."

"What about the dog?" She already knew the answer.

Joe glanced at Jack-Jack, at their feet, tail wagging enthusiastically. Sam suspected he was in on this somehow. "I suppose I can be bribed into allowing him to stay."

Sam couldn't help it, she made a little squealing noise, threw her arms around Joe's neck, and kissed him.

It was long and deep, and then Joe broke away, steadying her as he reached for her crutches. "Let's go."

"Where?" Sam shifted her weight to accept them and Jack-Jack barked, dancing at her feet.

"You can't possibly think I'm going to wait," Joe grinned cunningly. "I'm taking you to the courthouse and getting this finalized today."

She laughed. "We don't have a marriage license."

He went to a kitchen drawer and extracted something, sticking it in front of her of face so she could read it. "I pulled strings. Dupé owed me...*us*."

She looked at him in exasperation and shook her head. "What about Mom? We have to have her there. She'll kill me if we don't. And I'm on crutches. I shouldn't get married when I can't even stand on my own two feet."

He snuck in a quick kiss, and hustled her to the front door. "Val can meet us there. Crutches or no, I'm marrying you today."

Out into the sunny day they went, Jack-Jack bounding down the stairs and into the car. Sam couldn't keep the crazy smile off her face. How her life had turned around.

As Joe leaned down to buckle her seatbelt, she grabbed the front of his shirt and drew his face to hers. "I love you, Cahill. I always will."

Jack-Jack jumped in her lap and started licking both their faces.

Joe touched her chin, smiling as though he'd just won the lottery. "I love you, Rosenthal, soon to be Cahill. I always will."

The three of them drove to San Diego and the courthouse, ready to begin their new life together as a family.

ACKNOWLEDGMENTS

This book was inspired by a couple of things - one, my interest in bounty hunting after watching Dog, The Bounty Hunter, and his wife and family on their TV show. Beth Chapman, this is in loving memory of your patience and guidance to so many you encountered.

Secondly, I was stewing one night when I couldn't sleep about what it must be like to be a good guy (or gal) who's been falsely accused of terrorism. I had read an article about Quiet Skies, a real software program that targets air travelers, and my muse, who often enjoys working at 3 am, took over. The next morning when I sat down at my computer, I knew I had a story.

To those who helped bring this story to life, I'm forever grateful, and although I can't name you, I couldn't have written this as accurately without your input. Thank you!

As always, I'm grateful for my village of help - my hubby, kids, Princess Zoey and Princess Athena, as well as the real-life Thunder, who is always the inspiration for the Thunder in the SCVC Taskforce books.

Also to my street team, my editors, my betas, and my fellow

authors and friends who always lend an ear and inspiration when we're brainstorming.

A special thank you and a wink to JB Lynn, who told me to go with Deadly Bounty for the title when I was thinking of calling it Deadly Hunt instead. Nothing like confirmation from the Universe about a book title when you're standing in the paper towel aisle at the grocery store!

Finally, my undying love to all the fans of the taskforce series. Cooper, Celina, and the gang only exist because of YOU.

ROMANTIC SUSPENSE & MYSTERIES BY MISTY EVANS

SEALS of Shadow Force Series: Spy Division

Man Hunt

Man Killer

Man Down

SEALs of Shadow Force Series

Fatal Truth

Fatal Honor

Fatal Courage

Fatal Love

Fatal Vision

Fatal Thrill

Risk

The SCVC Taskforce Series

Deadly Pursuit

Deadly Deception

Deadly Force

Deadly Intent

Deadly Affair, A SCVC Taskforce novella

Deadly Attraction

Deadly Secrets

Deadly Holiday, A SCVC Taskforce novella

Deadly Target

Deadly Rescue

Deadly Bounty

The Super Agent Series

Operation Sheba

Operation Paris

Operation Proof of Life

Operation: Lost PrICess

The Justice Team Series (with Adrienne Giordano)

Stealing Justice

Cheating Justice

Holiday Justice

Exposing Justice

Undercover Justice

Protecting Justice

Missing Justice

Defending Justice

SCHOCK SISTERS MYSTERY SERIES w/Adrienne Giordano

1st Shock

2nd Strike

3rd Tango

The Secret Ingredient Culinary Mystery Series

The Secret Ingredient, A Culinary Romantic Mystery with Bonus Recipes

The Secret Life of Cranberry Sauce, A Secret Ingredient Holiday Novella

PNR & UF BY MISTY/NYX

Paranormal Romance

Witches Anonymous Step 1

Jingle Hells, Witches Anonymous Step 2

Wicked Souls, Witches Anonymous Step 3

Dark Moon Lilith, Witches Anonymous Step 4

Dancing With the Devil, Witches Anonymous Step 5

Devil's Due, Witches Anonymous Step 6

Dirty Deeds, Witches Anonymous Step 7

Wicked Wedding, Witches Anonymous Step 8

Urban Fantasy

Revenge Is Sweet, Kali Sweet Urban Fantasy Series, Book 1

Sweet Chaos, Kali Sweet Urban Fantasy Series, Book 2

Sweet Soldier, Kali Sweet Urban Fantasy Series, Book 3

Sweet Curse, Kali Sweet Urban Fantasy Series, Book 4

Paranormal Romantic Suspense

Soul Survivor, Moon Water Series, Book 1

Soul Protector, Moon Water Series, Book 2

Cozy Mysteries (writing as Nyx Halliwell)

Sister Witches Of Raven Falls Mystery Series

Of Potions and Portents

Of Curses and Charms

Of Stars and Spells

Of Spirits and Superstition

Confessions of a Closet Medium Cozy Mystery Series

(Coming 2020)

Pumpkins & Poltergeists

Once Upon a Witch Cozy Mystery Series

(Coming 2020)

Psychic Sisters Cozy Mystery Series

(Coming 2021)

ABOUT THE AUTHOR

USA TODAY Bestselling Author Misty Evans has published fifty novels and writes romantic suspense, urban fantasy, and paranormal romance. She got her start writing in 4th grade when she won second place in a school writing contest with an essay about her dad. Since then, she's written nonfiction magazine articles, started her own coaching business, become a yoga teacher, and raised twin boys on top of enjoying her fiction career.

When not reading or writing, she enjoys music, movies, and hanging out with her husband, twin sons, and two spoiled puppies. A registered yoga teacher and Master Reiki Practitioner, she shares her love of chakra yoga and energy healing, but still hasn't mastered levitating.

Get free reads, all the latest news, and alerts about sales when you sign up for her newsletter at www.readmistyevans.com. To find out more about her holistic healing practice, please visit www.crystalswithmisty.com.

LETTER FROM MISTY

Hello Beautiful Reader!

Thank you for reading this book! It is an honor and a privilege to write stories for you.

I hope you enjoyed this book, and I'd like to ask a favor – would you mind leaving a review at your favorite retailer? I'd really appreciate it, and reviews help other readers find books they will love too.

If you'd like to learn about my other books, sales, and special promotions, please sign up for my newsletter at www.readmistyevans.com.

Grab special edition box sets and get new releases before they come out at retailers by visiting my direct buy website www.mistyevansbooks.com.

I also have a holistic business, Crystals With Misty, and invite you to check out my website www.crystalswithmisty.com for information on my services.

Last but not least, if you enjoy clean, cozy mysteries, visit my pen name www.nyxhalliwell.com to see those books!

Thank you and happy reading!
Misty